LAND OF THE FREE

LAND OF THE FREE

A NOVEL BY
WOODROW LANDFAIR

John,

Thanks for the consideration and courage.
Put a lot of miles into this- hope you enjoy the ride! Keep Rollin,

HARBINGER
BOOK GROUP, USA

Some words, phrases and themes in LAND OF THE FREE were drafted from prior works performed or released by Woodrow Landfair:
48 STATES OF STORIES, Copyright © 2007 Woodrow Landfair
ROAD WILD HERO, Copyright © 2008 Woodrow Landfair
48 LIVE, Copyright © 2008 Woodrow Landfair
HIGHWAYS AND A HERO, Copyright © 2012 Woodrow Landfair

Harbinger Book Group brings authors to speak at your live events and considers special rates for educational, fundraising, and bulk purchasers. For inquiries, email outreach@harbinger-books.com

Harbinger Book Group, USA
175 Varick St., 4th floor
New York, New York 10014

www.harbinger-books.com

First Edition

Library of Congress Cataloguing-in-Publication Data has been applied for.

ISBN 978-1-9405-0035-5

1 2 3 4 5 6 7 8 9 10

"Give me your tired, your poor,
Your huddled masses yearning to breathe free..."

Prologue

A row of round, white bulbs surrounds the dressing room mirror, blurring my vision. I don't recognize myself. I see the wide eyes of a runaway boy chasing after an open freight car. I see the tightened brow of a young soldier staring into the scope of a rifle. Then there are the unshaven cheeks of a hurricane survivor, the dry lips of a homeless man, the irreverent air of an outlaw. The glass offers not so much a reflection but a composite, a police artist's sketch of a larger-than-life desperado on the run.

I flip again through the script on my lap. The pages are filled with freedom fighters and big city mobsters, immigrants living in New York tenements, southern jailers and the wrongly accused. The Great Plains sprawl across its long descriptive passages. The lawlessness of what was once the Wild West hovers just above the page. I snap the script shut.

This is *supposed* to be the factual account of my life, and once upon a time it was. But with each performance, in each new town, I've bent the truth... to the point of permanent creases.

For publicity, for money, for fame, for the

1

inflation of my ego, for the advancement of my dreams and my dreams for others, I turned my life into the ridiculous stack of pages in my hands. None of this ever really bothered me before, but as I stare into the mirror, I can't recognize my face. I can't remember my past. My breaths quicken until finally I'm choking on the wind in my throat.

"Are you okay?" The woman doing my makeup stops suddenly and puts her hand on my shoulder. "What's going on?"

I steady my breaths. "I'm okay," I say. "I'm okay."

She powders her brush again.

On a sofa in the corner, the musician is tuning his guitar. He plays a blues riff.

"You alright over there?" he asks.

I nod.

He continues playing. "How's *this*? Use it for the soundtrack tonight?"

"It's fine." I don't look up. The make-up artist works on my forehead. I'm back to reading the script. There are blaring sirens, screeching tires and shouting police officers with guns drawn. Again my breaths quicken.

"Chin-up." The make-up artist traces her slender fingers beneath my jaw. She wraps a thin cotton towel around my neck to keep my shirt from getting dirty.

I continue reading, memorizing for the hundredth time the story I'm paid to perform. It talks about hope, about desperation, about love and heartache, about the American Dream, about being a self-made man.

"Keep still." The make-up artist puts her palm on my knee.

I swipe at her hand. A photographer crouches to snap a candid photo. His flashbulb blinds me.

"Get out of here, will you?" I point into his lens as I leap from my chair. "No pictures before the show!"

The photographer peers at me over his camera.

I fix the towel around my neck as I sit back down. "I know. It's your job. I'm sorry. I need to focus right now. I've got..." I glance at the white cinder walls. They seem to be closing in on me. No matter which way I turn, I still can't find a clock.

The guitarist stops strumming. "Three minutes," he says.

The photographer still hasn't moved.

"I've only got three minutes, I'm sorry," I say.

The make-up artist whispers for everyone to hear, "I think he's just a little nervous."

But she's wrong. This isn't stage fright.

The door opens and slams shut. The photographer leaves and the tour manager enters. He is bald and wears glasses. From behind him, the low roar of the waiting crowd sweeps into the room like a draft.

Wiping the sweat from his hairless head, he peers at his clipboard then at his wristwatch.

"You got two minutes. The theater is a madhouse," the tour manager says. "Capacity crowd." He adjusts his bifocals and looks at his watch again. "A minute and a half."

I stare at the mirror, my face like an out of focus watercolor painting.

"You ready, kid?" The tour manager squeezes the meat of my shoulders. "You give Michigan a good show."

I pick up my script again and give it a final quick

3

read as I walk to the curtain. I move slowly, flipping through the scenes as I walk.

I can't remember if this is something real or something I've invented for the show: I'm standing in the Mississippi River under the light of a full moon, the mud between my toes and the tide up to my knees.

Then I'm in the ill-lit basement of a New York City restaurant. A man puts his hands around my throat. He's choking me, demanding the truth. I can't breathe.

In a cell of a small-town jail somewhere in the Deep South, a man in a tattered suit shakes my hand and tells me he can fix everything: "Forget the facts. Just stick with the story."

I unwrap the towel from my neck and toss it to the floor. My shadow rises up the wall. It forms the smooth silhouette of a stranger. I reach out to touch it and am startled by the coarseness when my hand meets the brick. The script scatters onto the floor around a prop motorcycle.

Are these stories mine? Parts of my life I chose to forget? Or stories I invented? Can I remember my story? Can I remember the truth? Can I remember anything at all? Do I even know what month it is?

Yes. July.

And the date?

The second. No. The third.

How old am I?

Uh... Twenty-eight. Yes. Twenty-eight.

And where did I start?

Texas. Well... Austin, anyway.

And how long ago was it that I started living this way?

4

It was... How old was I when I started? ...I was twenty-three. Five years. *Just* five years? Christ, has it only been that long?

The guitarist begins the soundtrack on stage. The audience is waiting for me. I move through the shadowy passageway toward the spotlight and step through the curtain. The audience rises like a swelling sea, applauding as I lift the microphone from the stand. Just like that, their applause peaks and settles as they fall to their seats. They wait in silence, and I have no idea what to say.

It's time to tell the truth. I must. I have to. If only for myself. There are parts I can't recall, parts I can't discern from all my lies, parts that just don't make sense, parts that don't even seem believable. But I'll tell everything of the last five years. I'll tell it as accurately and as honestly as I can, just as it lives within me.

The beginning I do remember.

Chapter One

I was leaving town on a recently purchased used motorcycle. I barely knew how to ride it, so I wanted to get out on the open road before the evening traffic.

I rushed about my room, rubbing my hands across my freshly-buzzed head as I searched to find what I needed: three pairs of pants, five shirts, six pairs of socks, a sweatshirt, a toothbrush, a stick of deodorant. I grabbed my camera from the bare mattress and picked up two empty notebooks, a handful of pens, and a nationwide road atlas. I stuffed everything into two black backpacks.

The phone rang. I didn't answer. I'd stopped returning calls a week ago. Friends had been leaving messages of concern. One of my old mentors called to say I was a "confused young man." The words echoed between my ears over and over again. I was not a confused young man. I'd made a clear-headed decision to abandon the life I'd been living—even my name.

My former life had been one of vicarious athletic glory as a benchwarmer on a champion college baseball team. It had been a life of regimentation too, with the Navy paying my way through school as part of the ROTC program. I never did make my commission though. The hectic schedule of division-one baseball had all but made me a scofflaw within the Navy unit; albeit a very well-liked scofflaw. But by the time graduation came, baseball injuries had so damaged my back I couldn't even pass the military's medical boards. What was left for me was perhaps to continue on in the sports world as a coach, perhaps while extending my undergraduate studies into a master's degree of some kind. All my life though, I'd madly aspired toward just two professions: Major League Baseball player and Navy SEAL. Both dreams had always been statistically improbable but knowing now that they were downright *impossible*, the thought of staying at the university seemed an absolute bore.

On my knees in the center of the one-room studio, I filled the two backpacks with the few remaining things I had. I'd pawned everything the day before—the furniture, the stereo, the television, the microwave, my textbooks, even my NCAA National Championship ring; anything I could sell. Earlier that morning I hawked my car and sold most of my clothes to a secondhand store.

The unsellables—the dishes, the sheets, the old pairs of boxer shorts, my worn baseball and Navy uniforms, old photographs—they'd remain in the apartment stacked on the counter or the floor. My landlord would have to dispose of them.

I'd decided that I would live the story of a lifetime—an odyssey, an epic adventure, the stuff of boyhood dreams. I'd take to the road with a few dollars in gas money. I'd drive that motorcycle across the entire country, rub the soil of my homeland into my skin, absorb its people's sweat. Somewhere along the way I'd find a new life and a new identity that would command fame and fortune. I'd be strong and brave, bookish and street-smart, defiant but kind and generous. As I saw it in my mind, my years on the road would teach me a unique and valuable skill-set which would somehow help both mankind and myself. That was my destiny. I was stupid enough to be certain of it.

I just needed to leave. And *now*, before I lost my nerve.

I took one last look around the room, picked up my gear, and headed out, slamming the door behind me.

The landlord's yellow lab ran to my feet as I slid the apartment key into the mail slot. I gave her a pat on the head while ripping a note from my journal to leave on the apartment door. It was just a few words to explain my disappearance—the only ones I could think of.

"Left... to discover America."

Outside, the sun reflected off my navy-blue motorcycle helmet—its silver star stickers and its red-and-white strips of reflective safety tape shining and mirroring the sky. I was cloaked beneath a sweat-steeped t-shirt. Between the sun's heat and the humidity, I was covered with beads of perspiration from my face to my forearms, even to my feet, but I was too preoccupied to care.

I tried over and over to shift gears without stalling, all while trying to maintain my balance atop the motorcycle's leather saddle. It was futile. Right when I finally found the correct speed at which to release the clutch, my sweat-slick hand slipped off the lever entirely, jolting me a few feet forward as the bike and I fell to the asphalt.

For a moment, lying there on the hot pavement, I realized that I must be full-blown crazy. Either that or I'd painted myself into a real corner.

In any case, I was too emotionally invested to quit at this point, and I was undeniably too short on time to worry. So I climbed back to my feet and back onto the motorcycle. I fired it up… and putzed out of town in first gear, stalling at every stop sign, getting passed by speeding cars, and doing my best to balance the two backpacks crudely roped to my rear seat.

The two-lane highway curled between gold-capped wheat fields below thinly-stretched burnt-orange clouds, purple skies peeking through them.

Along the roadside, farmers rode tractors, cattle grazed in the sun-beaten grass, dilapidated wooden barns kneeled far away in fields, aged brick buildings lined the Main Street of an old cow town.

At a roadside filling station, a bearded man fueled his pickup truck. Miles down the road, a teenage kid fixed a flat tire while a second boy sat dumbly in the passenger seat.

Down a roadside trail, a young woman walked a horse, its hooves caked in mud and clomping with each step.

I wondered about these people's lives, wondering over and over how it might feel to be them, what life meant to them, what significance they sought in their lives, what gifts and curses they derived from their homeland. Could I live someone else's life? Even for a little while? Maybe, but only if I could abandon myself.

As I saw it, I was at the beginning of a new life and as such I had to try to forget all my old friends and histories. Those things had been wonderful and I already missed them. But if I was ever going to fully steep myself in new experience, it made sense that I'd have to expunge my soul of all previous life, as thoroughly as possible. That's why I'd kept my departure a secret. I'd planned it for months and had hit the road with only a few goodbyes. I would be the person all my old friends would wonder about. *'Whatever happened to him?'*

I stalled out six times during that first day, and I crashed the bike three times, losing my balance at slow speeds. With some new holes in my jeans and some new dents in the bike, I had managed only about a hundred miles of progress. The sun was already low in the sky, and it was time for me to find a place to sleep.

I turned onto one of the highway's unpaved offshoots. At my back, the sun sank in the sky. Ahead of me, a walnut orchard looked like a promising place to drop a sleeping bag. I turned onto a gravel path, grimacing as the motorcycle crashed to the ground again. The left rearview mirror snapped off, and both backpacks came untied from their ropes, slamming me in the back of the helmet.

Lying in the gravel, I surveyed my surroundings and let my ears unring. Barbwire cattle fences shouldered the narrow path, "No Trespassing" signs nailed to every tall post. America was owned, every piece of it. I had to be a fool setting out like I was. Perhaps the America of adventure for which I yearned was a thing of the past.

10

The trip I hoped for was starting to look like little more than a fantasy. I didn't know how to ride a motorcycle, first of all. And second, sleeping outside seemed fine in theory, but now that I was actually about to do it, it felt incredibly dangerous. Any passerby could have his way with me, and it wasn't like I'd have the police on my side. The sinking feeling in my spirits seemed to be telling me that my only asset was having nothing to lose. Perhaps I'd survive by putting my hands to labor. I didn't have any special skill or service to offer, just as I had no material goods to sell. What if I had to make my living on the fringes? In any case, turning back was not an option.

I dusted myself off and mounted the motorcycle again.

In the distance, the freight cars of a long train stretched along their tracks. A boy sprinted toward them as they began their slow crawl into motion. He appeared from a nearby farmhouse surrounded by walnut trees, a green John Deere in its dirt driveway. Over his shoulder, the boy carried a sack that bounced with each stride he took.

I was too far away to see what happened next, and lost sight of him through the walnut orchard's screen of branches. I didn't see him climb onto the train, but I've always assumed he made it. I wanted to believe it, even though it's possible he didn't. And it's also possible he was only pretending—simply play-acting the part of a runaway, maybe for the hundredth time.

I can see it in my mind, just as he may have imagined it too... the boy throws his bag on the car mid-stride and takes one more step before leaping toward the boxcar's open door. He strains to pull himself all the way in and crawls to his feet on the dusty floorboards. The boy stands and watches from the door as the familiar surroundings disappear.

Later, he lays down, using his sack for a pillow, knowing that when he wakes he'll be in a new town with new people. The breeze of the open door ruffles through his hair. The miles roll away below his head. He feels like he left his old life behind, like he's transformed into a new, blank self. He wonders what will become of his life. Then a smile appears on his face. He is on the move—as free as the air in the sky.

I woke up in my sleeping bag in some roadside field, the motorcycle at my side, a rock beneath its kickstand to keep it from sinking into the soil.

I knew I crossed into Arkansas. I had spent time watching people, listening-in on conversations at roadside cafes, riding on back roads trying to figure out exactly how I would provide for myself.

In a northern Arkansas pizza joint, I inquired about a help-wanted sign in the window. I was immediately turned away; they said they only wanted someone who'd worked in a restaurant before.

That made me realize the importance of having a powerful story. I could try to continue convincing people that I could do the work... or I could move them to help out an adventurer in the middle of an odyssey... or, hell, I could tell them anything they wanted to hear. If I was friendly enough and framed myself well and told a good tale, and found some legitimate way to add value to someone's day, I could probably land a different job in every town. I could be a janitor in one place and a sales clerk in another. I could be all sorts of different folks. All I needed to do was weave enough yarn to score some jobs. I could go everywhere, be anyone. I could live a life of infinite experience. It was an idea, a philosophy of sorts, which I embraced without question.

It's around this point that my mind starts to get fuzzy, not from any lack of remembrances, but from a surplus of disjointed scenes. Whether these memories are real, or embellishments, or complete fabrications, I may never know for sure.

Chapter Two

All I see is the blinding white of the spotlight. All I feel is the microphone in my sweaty palm and all I have to offer the audience is the silence of my confused mind. Where was I?

I shut my eyes and see myself as a college-age male traveling across green farmlands: mornings squinting against the yellow sunrise, afternoons with the sun burning my neck, nights spent slapping the mosquitoes from my skin. Time's a blur.

At an Arkansas produce stand, I'm eating watermelon under a cloudless sky. Two hours south of Little Rock, I'm camping in the darkness of a tall pine forest. Just off Highway 412, a woman in a minivan is asking me where I'm headed. A butcher at a grocery store in Bentonville tells me jokes. I'm working the register there.

In Texarkana, I'm hauling boxes at a loading dock.

In Pine Bluff, I'm cooking short order at a diner.

In some town I can't recall, I'm selling fireworks at a roadside shack.

I remember sitting at a bar in a Fayetteville Days Inn. A clean-shaven man at the next stool was mentioning a state teachers' convention.

"Let me guess," he said, furrowing his brow in concentration. "P.E.?"

"Huh?" I responded.

"You teach Phys Ed, right? I can always tell."

I cocked my head to the side and gave him a wink. "You guessed it."

He told me he teaches high school science. "Do you know what room our buffet's in?"

"No," I said, but I doubled back. "*We* should go look."

We found the dining room together. I glanced at the hostesses' guest list and used one of the names as I looked her in the eyes and introduced myself.

"Here you are, sir." She handed me a nametag for "Mr. Morgan, Physical Education, Jonestown Middle School." I stuck it to my chest and followed the other teachers to our free meal.

As I sat down with my plate, the hotel manager tapped me on the shoulder, her acrylic fingernails pressing against my shirt.

"Excuse me sir, but we have someone *else* under that name." She flicked my nametag.

I looked up, biting my lip as the hostess stared back at me. A man in khakis and a sport coat watched from beside her, raising his eyebrows and shaking his head.

The manager leaned over me, swiping the napkin from my lap. "Care to tell us who you really are?"

In a lot of ways, I was a different person to everyone I met. In a Batesville field, I befriended a homeless man and asked him about places to sleep. He gave me a handful of suggestions. I thanked him.

"No problem," he said. "We homeless brothers gotta stick together."

On a rainy night in Fairfield, I showed an elderly couple in an RV park how to set up their grill. They shared dinner with me.

"It's always nice to meet other campers," the old woman said.

In a Sheridan dancehall, I helped wipe the floor after a woman spilt her drink.

The band's manager yelled to me over the speaker volume from the side of the stage. "You work here, right?"

"What?"

"Can you help us clear the equipment at the end of the show?" he said.

I unplugged the amps and loaded the guitar cases into their van. The band thought I was one of the bartenders. They brought me to their after-party. We took round after round of shots in their motel room. They let me crash there.

Paying for fuel in a West Helena general store, I reached beneath the counter after dropping my wallet. A young man with a whitewall military haircut bent to grab it. Peering over my shoulder, he stared into the parking lot.

"Is that your motorcycle out there?" he said.

I nodded.

"I've always wanted one a'those. Can I take a

look?"

Ten minutes later we were inside a saloon down the street. I told him I couldn't afford to buy too many drinks.

He nodded at my ROTC haircut and gave me a wink. He turned to the bartender.

"A round for me and my buddy here before we get shipped out tomorrow."

The bartender handed us two free beers, returning with refills whenever the mugs went dry.

"Another round for the troops!" the bartender kept announcing.

My new friend—twenty-one years-old, white, lean build, brown hair—was back on leave in his hometown for a few days before deployment.

It was past midnight by the time we were walking back to his weatherworn, dented Camaro, the parking lot loud and full of headlights as the beer joints closed for the night.

He offered to take me back to the motorcycle, but I declined. He insisted there was something we had to do, so we drove across a bridge over a wide body of water just east of town.

"We need to swim!" He was shouting over the sound of the air rushing through the open windows. The needle on the dashboard's speedometer was dancing around eighty.

He caught me staring at the water. I'd been in West Helena so briefly I'd failed to realize the significance of the water on its eastern border.

"The Mississippi River!" he shouted, pointing out his window into the foggy haze.

He sped to the end of the structure then swerved to the shoulder, the gravel kicking up from beneath the tires as he skidded to a stop. He opened the door and slammed it behind him. I followed as he stumbled down the shoulder and through the darkness.

"God, why didn't I think of this before?" he said, the words slipping from his lips. He was hammered, the last few shots still hitting him. "This is perfect. The Mississippi River, by God, nothing more patriotic than that. You know practically the whole country drains into it. Like the nation's sink." He went on and on. "Bet the bottom's red, white, and blue."

He staggered toward the bridge. I tried to stop him, but he was loud and determined.

"God! Why didn't we think of this before? It's perfect. You know, really. Like everything in this whole country washes into it... and then washes out into the Gulf of Mexico, the Panama Canal, the Atlantic, *and* the Pacific Oceans... the entire world."

His body jolted like he'd gotten hit in the chest with a bat.

"Fenced off! Damned thing's fff..." He slapped a mosquito from his neck, and he was silent for a moment.

"Who the...? They can't—it's *our* river! *Our* river." He was jabbing his thumb against his chest. "Our river!" he stammered and hurried back to the car.

He refused to give me the keys. He turned the ignition, and we raced down the highway, swerving across two lanes to the nearest exit.

"Fenced off? You're *kidding* me. It's our right to swim in that river." The Chevy sped through residential streets.

I leaned out the window as he rambled.

"It's our *duty* to swim in that river. We call ourselves Americans?"

He slowed the old sports car at every few driveways to see if he could make out the river between rows of houses. The unlit windows reflected the streetlights.

"It's ab*surd*! Ridicu... Every person, every American should be made to... To earn citizenship every person in America, fourth graders, throw 'em in... make it a mandatory social studies credit." The car swerved as he took his hands off the wheel to gesticulate. "Throw them in. Everyone. Just throw 'em in!"

He grabbed the wheel again, and my shoulder banged against the door as he corrected the steering. He shook his head, searching for words.

I interjected every few minutes, trying to keep him under control but he was blabbering on and on, waving his hands like a madman and weaving all over the road because of it.

"Like, like... a ..." He slapped his thigh, still deep in his own thoughts. "Baptism! ...An American baptism."

He made a hard left turn. The speedometer spiked as he hit the gas.

He slammed on the breaks. The seatbelt dug into my chest.

"That's it!" he screamed, pointing out my window, over the lawn of a waterfront home and into the fog.

He threw open the door, stood, and undressed to his shorts, still lecturing me on how the Mississippi River was once the lifeblood of this country, the economic backbone of the west all the way until the early twentieth century, how the river is somehow connected ecologically with every being on earth... and on and on and on.

"Hey," he said, slamming his door. He was shiny with sweat and breathing hard. "I'm leaving the keys in the ignition." he explained, shaking his finger at me, "just in case."

He sprinted into the mist.

I ran after him and threw off my shirt. At the edge of the yard, he came to a halt. I slammed bare-chested against his sweaty back.

We stood at the top of a seawall, the house behind us quiet and still as a sleeping baby.

"Come on!" I shouted in a whisper, pulling on his shoulder. "Let's get outta here."

He shoved me and held a finger over his lips. "Shh! You'll get us busted!"

He turned and climbed down onto large rocks. Again I followed, the boulders slick with algae. I stepped into mud. We were up to our ankles then to our shins. We kept walking until we reached water.

My toe smashed against a sharp rock.

"Ah!" I cursed loudly. My words echoed over the water. "I think I broke it!" I shouted before coming to my senses.

We stood in silence, the echo subsiding.

A light turned on in a window. Then a light on the porch. The backdoor opened with a screech. A silhouette stood in the doorway and called into the darkness.

"What's going on out here?"

We didn't respond.

The homeowner walked onto the lawn with a flashlight.

"What the hell's going on?" He waited, standing in the middle of his yard. He was holding something long over his shoulder—a baseball bat? a rifle?

My friend pointed to the mud below us, made a throwing motion with his arm, and pointed to the left side of the house. He made a running motion then pointed to the right. I understood.

Quickly we reached down, scooping the brown mud, shaping it into spheres. Then we threw them as hard as we could and paused in silence waiting to hear the sound of the mud splattering against the house. But instead we heard only a sudden groan. Then a loud scream that didn't stop as we lifted each other over the seawall and sprinted across the lawn.

As we made our getaway, I saw that our throws had been horribly off target. One landed on the man's leg, the other on his face.

We spotted the Camaro's shiny steel bumper as we darted across the lawn. Our mud-slick hands slipping on the handles of the car doors, I took the driver's seat without realizing. My bloody toe seethed. The homeowner ran into the street trying to get a good look at us just as we sped off.

High on adrenaline and sober with fear, we soared across the open road. With one hand on the radio and the other packing a tin of Copenhagen, the soldier talked about driving on and never turning back. For a few hours, I drove due west, the two of us talking. The soldier had a deployment to prepare for and a fiancé to see for a farewell dinner. He described her—thin, tall, blonde, a college student. I saw them clearly: he making good on his dream of becoming a war hero, living in the barracks of some faraway base, in a tent at some distant war zone; she at a sorority house or dorm room. At daybreak, we turned around and headed back. The soldier got behind the wheel, and we moved southeasterly through the stubby cliffs of northwest Arkansas. I looked at him as he drove. Eyes on the road, he talked about secret sexual desires and worst fears and the dormant dreams of his childhood. The old Chevy purred down the highway.

A motorcycle approached from behind.

Train tracks ran parallel to the road, and a long train rolled by, its boxcar doors wide open.

For a while, the three machines shared one direction.

They split at a curve in the ridge: The soldier steered the Chevy around the hill, the long train disappeared into a tunnel, and the motorcycle chugged noisily up the steep road, approaching the stormy clouds of a blossoming morning.

Chapter Three

Picture a man on a motorcycle speeding through the hill country of northern Arkansas, continuing into the distance mile after mile until he's nothing more than a spec on the horizon, motoring through Foley, Alabama, and crossing into the panhandle of Florida.

Squinting against a pouring rain, the traveler slows carefully on the slick streets and turns into the first open parking lot.

Shivering in an air-conditioned diner, he forks hot apple pie and ice cream and warms himself with a cup of black coffee.

Sitting up late in a motel bed, he stares out the window.

Driving into the morning sun, he watches oranges dance from the branches of trees, their trunks sprouting in rows on either side of the highway. With a strobe-effect, the daylight passes through the orchards and the trees appear like drawings in a flipbook.

Holed up in a Dade City motel room as the rain falls, the man flips channels on a blurry television.

He's hit-on in a country western bar. He takes a job at a fried chicken joint, but quits. He's mugged by a gang of hoodlums. He cries alone on the sands of

Daytona Beach in the rain.

Labor Day, Halloween, and Christmas came and went. The Fourth of July was fast approaching. That's when I found myself just outside of Brunswick, Georgia without money in my pocket for gas.

In the parking lot of a hardware depot, I anchored the motorcycle. I secured the backpacks to the bike with twine to make it less tempting for someone to take them. They contained just my old clothes, my camera, my beat-up laptop computer, a simple cell phone that had been dead for weeks, some notebooks, and a sleeping bag—those possessions were all I had.

Across the parking lot, I joined a group of Latino men waiting to get picked up for day labor. Many of them wore pants stained white from paint. Some held hammers. Others held shovels. I ran my hand across my weeklong beard and stared at the ground. A few men spoke softly in quick beats of Spanish.

Six of us were picked by the first truck that drove by. It was a blue long-bed Ford.

"You, you, you, you, you and..." The contractor ran his finger down the line of men. "You." He stopped with his finger pointed at my sun burnt face.

I grimaced but tried to hide my limp as I stepped forward. My toe had been infected for weeks and it had swollen to the size of a golf ball. It pressed painfully against the inside of my boot. I climbed into the back of the Ford with the other men. We rumbled down the highway, warm morning sun on our faces, cool wind in our hair. Loose hammers and shovels slid along the truck bed with every turn.

At the job-site, we hauled lumber up the driveways of houseless yards. When the boss yelled "Clavos!" I scrambled back to the truck for the bucket of nails.

With calloused hands, we hammered. With stiff backs, we lifted. As I climbed up to what would be the second story of a house, a fellow worker warned me in Spanish. "Careful," he said as he handed me an armload of two-by-fours. "You get hurt, no one pay."

The sun set against our tired eyes, and we piled back into the bed of the pickup truck and counted the cash in our hands. We rumbled again down the blacktop to the hardware store and leapt from the vehicle. One of the workers asked the others for a ride to the beach, where he planned to sleep for the night. It was the best idea I could think of.

"Get up," a man yelled from behind his flashlight. I heard waves crash in the darkness.

"Ya can't sleep here," shouted another voice. A boot sent sand in my face.

The coarse particles stung my eyes. As I re-opened them, the flashlight blinded me.

Two officers were pulling at my sleeping bag, kicking sand at me.

"You speak English?" one of them shouted. They demanded I gather my things, and they followed me off the beach.

"You're lucky you're not going to jail for vagrancy," one officer continued as I walked to the motorcycle. "Don't come back."

I drove into the night, my mind cloudy with fatigue.

Somewhere I was sleeping peacefully in a warm bed. Somewhere I was safe in the comfort of a home.

Somewhere I was a worried father waiting for my son to return. Somewhere I was running my love-hungry hands up the back of my sweetheart, sweeping her long hair off her bare skin, our mouths linked in passion.

My bike moved through the damp midnight of the land, through the many fogs of my environment. I was a gas station attendant working a graveyard shift. I was a schoolteacher staying up late grading exams. I was an exhausted mother finishing the last load of laundry.

I was an excited college student running off with a secret lover in the middle of the night, clothes spilling from unzipped luggage. I hopped into my lover's old blue convertible and we drove, New York City bound. The night was hot, the breeze warm. We talked about maybe going out west, but we swore that whichever way we headed we'd never turn back.

I was a trucker sipping coffee, staring through an eighteen-wheeler's bug-splattered windshield toward an endless strip of black pavement. A red hue reflected off the golden water and onto the highway.

My memory grew vague, rising and receding as the Carolina tides. The lives I witnessed blurred with all the lives I had led.

The motorcycle roared. With no one on the road, I covered implausible mileage. Time was a mystery, and identity was an unanswerable riddle.

Wherever I was, whoever I was, I was traveling.

Every town held something new: a new place, a new job,

a new life.

I was a tramp, often working short labor stints—routing water lines in farm fields, for instance. My sweat-soaked t-shirt, sour-smelling under the midsummer sun, covered the aching muscles of my shoulders, bruised from lugging heavy pipes.

Occasionally, I went door-to-door asking for work and would find myself splitting firewood or loading moving vans.

I was a gas station attendant. I was a janitor at a bus station. I was given room and board in an antebellum mansion in exchange for farm work. I was taken in by families and treated as a brother.

Once, in Macon, I filled in as an auctioneer: *I got five hear six, six-fifty here? Six-twenty-five, six-fifty, seven hundred? Do-I-have-seven-got-seven-man-in-the-red-hat. Seven-once-twice-sold! Sold, to the man in the red hat, seven-hundred!*

For a week in Marietta, I fed a family with my auction checks and spent the rest of my money alone at the dog tracks in the afternoons.

In Greenwood, I was an old man splitting my time between whiskey and bridge.

In Orangeburg, I was a store clerk living with a brother in a doublewide trailer. I was a tan surfer boy in Myrtle Beach, an olive-skinned innkeeper in Winston-Salem. And all too often, I was a rambling hobo—welcomed-into and kicked-out-of almost every home and motel south of the Mason Dixon line.

Bleached by the sun, eroded by the waves, ripped by the gales, and deafened by the whistle of the ever-departing train, my windblown soul seemed to absorb the lives around me, empathizing with everyone I met, seeing life on their terms, through their eyes.

In Roanoke, I was a bible-belt minister. Arriving to work early one Sunday, I found a man sleeping in the parking lot.

"Let me take you to breakfast," I said. "You've lost your way." I stared at the bearded man as he silently gathered his backpacks, securing them with a roll of twine.

"God has a plan for each of us," I tried again.

Paying me no mind, he unbuckled a saddlebag and dropped a jar of peanut butter inside.

"...a confused young man," I mumbled to myself, and I walked alone into my church.

The preacher disappeared inside the chapel. I strapped my sleeping bag to the motorcycle. My shirt was sticky in the morning humidity. My moist skin, several days unwashed, was brown with dirt.

I sat on the motorcycle eating a peanut butter sandwich. The preacher appeared again in the doorway, and walked toward me.

"I can't let you leave without speaking to you about the Lord. Not in good conscience I can't." His shoes pattered against the sand as he came closer. "Do you know anything about love? About healing?"

I tongued the sticky remainder of peanut butter at the roof of my mouth.

"How can you live like this? Do you have a family? Isn't there anyone who cares about you?"

The preacher looked curiously at my two book bags, and the tattered ropes that held them to the worn motorcycle. I continued packing.

"You can know peace. You can know love. You can know *God.*"

I watched the preacher's wrinkle-less face.

"Have you ever felt love?" he asked. "I mean, have you? Have you ever felt really loved by someone?"

I looked at his moving lips, his eyes, his cheeks, his hair.

"What if you knew that the whole universe cares for you?" he continued.

Over his shoulder, the open road and a lone car receded into the distance.

"Do you..." He paused as he formulated his question. "Do you know what it feels like to have someone really love you?"

I was a lifeguard at a Virginia country club. The smell of sunscreen mixed with the scent of floral perfume. Lawn chairs circled the pool. A whistle spun on a lanyard around my finger, dark shades covered my eyes. I tanned on the guard stand with a towel over my swimsuit. The sun disappeared behind dark clouds.

"One bounce on the board!" I shouted after a tweet on the whistle.

A boom of thunder and a crack of lightning pierced the darkening sky. I blew the whistle again. "Clear the water!"

Taking refuge in the guard office, I watched the clouds empty onto the land.

A young blonde ran across the deck. She swept the wet curls from her eyes, licked the drops of water from her mouth, rubbed a pink finger-nailed hand across her thin nose.

Bending to grab a towel from the stack by my chair, as if recognizing a familiar musk, she slowly stood, her nose within inches of my shirtless body. A drop of rain hung on her lashes as she looked at me with almond eyes.

Mornings, she came to watch me sweep the decks. Afternoons, she brought me lunch. Evenings, we walked by moonlight hand in hand on the winding paths of the golf course. I pulled her close, rubbing the back of her neck with one hand, sweeping the tangle of loose buttery curls from her face with the other.

At night—on the manicured fairways of the golf course, on her soft mattress in her bedroom, on the wood floors of her parents' living room when no one else was home—our bodies shared a pulse. We'd lie on our backs and never speak of who we'd been, never of who we might become.

I sensed tension in her breath. Then I felt her fragility wrap around me.

"What are you thinking?" She asked as she peeled herself from my body.

She stood, her hair falling to her nipples. She placed a hand on her hip, her velvety legs stretching to the floor, and reached for a bottle of water.

I told her I was happy.

She swore it would never end.

Keg parties at her friends' apartments... A night under the stars during an unforgettable weekend at the rented beach house of her classmates... A lust-filled fifteen minutes in the pool office on a rainy evening... Cocktail

hours at the country club... A garden party on a sun-
bleached afternoon... The Fourth of July, watching
fireworks together on the national mall... A late
summer's argument dragging past dusk, two lovers
crying in the dark.

Fall was coming, her academic year about to start.
I'd been offered long-term employment. She knew I'd
turned it down.

On a humid August morning, we carried boxes and
duffels from her front door. The blacktop driveway was
hot under my bare feet as I dropped luggage into her
trunk.

She packed the backseat, placing food and clothes
across the floor.

"I'll transfer. Something close by," she said,
hugging me. "My mom says..."

I walked around her, tossing the bags into her car,
eyeing the road over her shoulder.

I loaded the boxes of skirts and jackets, shirts and
shoes.

Her cheeks dripped with tears, her lashes shiny
and wet. She held me. She kissed me. She filled herself
with promises of reunion.

I brushed past her as I slid a final bag into the
trunk.

"What's so important to you that we can't..." she
paused, "so important that you need to go out and do it
with*out* me?"

I was looking at the asphalt, my bottom lip
between my teeth. Her face was warm against my
cheek, blushing red as I pulled away.

"Tell me," she repeated. "What's that important to

31

you?"

I was so used to leaving... For me it was easy.

Why then, as she left to return to school and I left to return to the road, did it feel like my heart had just been ripped from my chest?

The microphone is still at my lips. I can hear myself breathing over the stage monitors and behind that I hear the audience's faint whispers growing louder each second I stall. The memory is too painful. I can't continue. I wish only to escape but I must say something.

I close my eyes and picture that boy stowed away on that freight train. He is slouched against a wall, half-asleep, having already passed through who-knows-how-many states.

A bang on the boxcar floor startles him. He sits up, his heart racing. A canvas seabag has been tossed through the open door. Small clouds of dust rise from the wood around it. The train is picking up speed.

Loud footsteps—boots over sandstone—stamp outside in harmony with the chugging of the engine and the cacophonous percussion of steel wheels against steel tracks. A pair of weathered hands slap onto the boards of the open car. A grizzled, bearded man grunts as he lifts himself onto the moving train.

The boy scoots to the far wall, his mouth open, his breaths heavy.

A second seabag plops onto the deck. A second pair of hands plants themselves onto the floorboards as a second man pulls himself into the car.

The two men flop exhaustedly to their stomachs,

their heavy breathing clouding the dusty floor. One of them looks up and sees the boy.

"Hey," the first man says as he crawls to his feet. He walks to the opposite wall.

The boy stands shaky-legged, his wounded toe throbbing. He strains to keep his face taut and tough.

"It's alright little guy. We ain't gonna hurt you."

The other man rises and walks around the rattling freight car.

He stares at the boy. "How long you been on, kid?"

The boy looks at the ragged men.

"Don't wanna talk to strangers, eh?" one says with a laugh.

"Well how 'bout this then?" The man unlatches the top of a drab green seabag, unwrapping the canvas folds. He reaches in and brings out a plastic sack, a loaf of bread inside.

"Here ya go. Have yourself somethin' to eat."

His hand shakes nervously as he accepts two slices.

"Hungry little feller, ain't ya? Not to worry, plenty more."

The three sit down together against the filthy wood-lined walls, using their baggage for pillows while they chat, laugh, and nap. One of the men withdraws a jug of whiskey from his bag. The boy holds out his open hand. The man looks at him suspiciously but gives him the bottle. The boy removes his boot and sock and spills a dash of the brown liquor on his infected toe. He exhales slowly, wincing as the alcohol burns. He closes his eyes and presses his back against the wall.

At each town, more men crawl in. The boxcar gets

more crowded by the hour, and the conversations get louder as the miles roll on, each person taking a turn to share his story.

And when it becomes the boy's turn to talk—sitting in the center of the circle, watching the men rolling smokes or swigging from whiskey flasks—the boy tells the tale of a broken-hearted man who chose the road over his sweetheart. A lonely man knew nothing else, and searched for any far off place. A lost soul set back out to learn about his homeland but questioned his decision to stay on the road.

Chapter Four

In southern Maryland, I lived in a shack along the Patuxent River, eating the crabs I could trap and fish I could string on a line. I travelled north to Delaware where I parked cars as a restaurant valet. In Lancaster I worked as a repairman. In Pittsburgh I joined striking steel workers on a picket line.

I headed north through Pennsylvania then east through New Jersey. I delivered pizza in Asbury Park. I lived with a longshoreman near Port Elizabeth, but before long, I set out again on the motorcycle. I came to Manhattan looking for work and came to the homeless shelter after I'd failed to find any.

Bellevue's halls smelled heavily of old tomato soup. In the waiting room, I sat across from a man in an old suit, threadbare at the knees and stained at the armpits. Another man slouched close-eyed in a chair across the room. He was shoeless, reeked of urine, and may have been unconscious.

An old white man, his face beneath a few weeks' gray beard, handed me a small bag of pretzels. He gave another to a black kid one chair over.

He said he'd gotten them from a drugstore.

We thanked him and ate slowly, our stomachs too

empty to eat quickly.

In a private cubicle, I sat before an inquisitive social worker reading from a card.

"Do you understand that you are not required to answer any of these questions but that any information you can give us will help us serve you?"

I nodded. She continued.

"You can leave the shelter at anytime. We cannot hold you here against your will. Do you understand?"

I nodded. She continued.

The black haired woman behind the desk took a photo. She inked my thumbs. In black and white, she printed my mug shot on an eight-and-a-half by eleven sheet of paper along with my thumbprints and an assigned nine-digit number.

She called this my meal ticket and handed it to me along with a subway pass and directions from the Lower East Side to the Atlantic Avenue Homeless Shelter in Brooklyn.

I followed a group of other recently registered homeless to a subway station nearby.

We said nothing on the train. All of us looked enviously at the one man who wore a proper coat. I wrapped my arms around my chest and leaned over my knees. The train shook against the rails into Brooklyn.

Behind the shelter's metal detectors, two dozen of us filled a fifteen-chair room. Those without seats sat on the cement. Another black kid—good looking, poised, and carrying a red, white, and blue helmet of some sort—stood from his seat and offered me his chair.

A familiar-looking old-timer in the corner griped about the wait.

The man next to me leaned to whisper in my ear. "That guy comes in every few days and always complains about how long this takes." He—white, mid-thirties, and dressed in shorts, a bathrobe, and house-slippers—sipped casually on a Styrofoam cup of coffee while unfolding the newspaper on his lap.

"I'm already registered," he said. "I just come down and watch the new guys roll in at night."

I nodded.

"That guy has to come here as part of his parole," he whispered with a gesture at a gray bearded man in a ripped sweater. "He gets to go home after he checks in."

"That guy," he pointed to a black man in a wheelchair, "says he lost the use of his legs in the war." He shook his head and shrugged. "He's got a Purple Heart. Keeps it in his back pocket."

The old-timer saw me studying the face of a young man across the room.

"That guy ran away from home as a kid." He looked to be twenty-something and wore mud-stained denim and a black sweatshirt bleached gray by the sun. "Trouble with his dad."

"Me," he continued, "I've been here since September."

His speech slowed and he stared at the floor. He rested his head in his hands breathing heavily.

I leaned to the other side of my chair.

The man to my left gave a nudge and whispered in my ear. "Don't listen to him." He shook his head. "The guy's nuts."

A uniformed worker entered from a doorway in the corner.

One by one, we were called to our room assignments. The workers addressed us by the numbers on our meal tickets.

Men were still entering the holding area when I was called and pointed to a bed. My room was that of thirty-nine others—twenty cots lined up on opposite walls.

In the darkness of morning, I woke to a hacking cough in the opposite bed. A man in boxer shorts walked to a lit hallway, his shoes clip-clopping on a cement floor.

Three beds down, a man sat staring at the wall. Five beds from him, a black man—his shirt off and his belly resting on his lap—scratched furiously at his torso. Another loud cough echoed through the room.

I slid out from under a wool blanket and sandpaper-stiff cotton sheets. The mattress beneath me rustled against its plastic cover.

In the bathroom—bleach fumes so heavy it was hard to breathe—I splashed water on my face.

A man next to me brushed his teeth with an issued white toothbrush.

"No hot water in this place," he said as he strained to twist the knob.

He finished brushing his teeth and stood over a trashcan, emptying his pockets into the basket. His toothbrush dangled from his lips like a cigarette as he studied the items in his pockets before throwing them away—a torn piece of paper, a busted pen, an old subway pass, an empty pack of menthol smokes, and a half-eaten candy bar in a brown gooey wrapper. I stared at the melted chocolate oozing from the plastic. I took extra time to wash my face. As soon as the man left, I looked around to see if anyone would see me and walked over to the trashcan.

Outside the shelter, a few coveted bottles of three-dollar wine were passed around.

On a stoop nearby, the leather-faced man who slept next to me read his bible aloud to five shivering souls.

I sat down on the curb and cried. A gray haired black man asked me if I had some spare change for subway fare into Manhattan.

I tried to hide the tears on my cheeks as I fished through the pockets of my jeans.

He mumbled, "I'll give it back tomorrow. At breakfast. A dime? Anything? I'm going over there to get a... oh, thank you, brother."

I handed him the coins.

"I know I can find a job over there," he continued his voice wavering almost maniacally. "I struck out yesterday but I got a good feelin' about today. Job's waitin' for me."

We were outcasts by our own fault, by others' faults, by fate, and by our own feeble will. We were winners down on our luck, delusional religious prophets, and born losers all sleeping in a room like animals in a stable.

We were too low on life's slope to see past the next horizon. Every dollar we spent was our last, every sunrise another miracle. The addicted and the abused— they envied those weak enough to die.

For the most part, we were willing to help one another. As a group we stood side by side. But never did we trust anyone—not even our own kind. We slept lightly, never too asleep to defend ourselves at the slightest threat. No one left his belongings out of reach. But many of us went out of our way to share with our peers. Men with pocket change offered it to those without. Those who read books in the cafeteria at breakfast passed the finished paperbacks to those who wanted them.

On October 31st, my third full day in New York City, I was hired under trumped-up references to check IDs at a nightclub.

A week later, on Election Day, I worked for fourteen dollars an hour handing out campaign pamphlets all around the city.

Everyone in Manhattan wore a costume. In the East Village, the mohawked and the nose ringed adorned themselves in tight jeans strapped with chain belts. They were tattooed, pierced, bleached, and dyed.

In the West Village, flower-dressed twenty-somethings masqueraded as hippies. Guitar slinging hipsters posed as folk musicians.

Times Square covered itself in advertisements and paraded under flashing lights.

Downtown, clean-shaven and slick-haired gentlemen hid behind dark suits and power ties.

In SoHo, lanky girls strutted the sidewalks as if on a runway. At the street corners and subway stations, men claiming to be Jesus preached to inattentive pedestrians pretending to be too busy to listen.

No one was who he claimed to be. Everyone had a story.

I invented credentials to get bartending and waiting jobs. I created histories as a carpenter to secure handyman work. I slept in a friend's garage in Queens, on a mattress beside a space heater beneath a bare light bulb and a single electric socket. I had a bed, a sleeping bag, my backpacks, and a place to stash the bike. I washed and shaved in the sinks of McDonald's restrooms to maintain a well-groomed appearance for job interviews. Sometimes an angry manager required me to make an order first.

On Christmas Eve and into Christmas morning, I guarded the VIP section at a Jewish singles party.

For a week, I managed to work as the super at an apartment building, fixing drain clogs and electrical shorts, even making an eviction. ("Don't complain to me you don't have the money. You're three weeks late already!") But my inexperience was obvious to every tenant in the building, and I quickly moved on.

I worked as a room-service bellhop at a five-star hotel, as a night watchman at the Port Authority Bus Station, and as a crate builder at an art studio.

Desperate for a good meal, I posed as a stockbroker at a Wall Street Convention Dinner.

"Yes, sir. I see the name on the list..." The manager shook his head.

I threw up my arms in protest. "I just told your hostess; my luggage, my wallet, my suit bag—they all got lost at the airport."

"Not this time, sir." The manager stretched the velvet rope across the doorway, watching me with satisfaction as I turned to leave.

I slept in subway cars, on the carpet of a

musician's apartment, in the beds of coworkers, and on the wood floor living room of a police officer I met moonlighting as a dance-club doorman. Many nights I slept on couches in the upper floors of the NYU library, my face buried between the pages of a literature textbook, my hand clutching a student ID I'd found on 7th Avenue.

For a few days, I shared a closet-sized room with two artists in a flophouse on St. Mark's Place. In Astoria, I was given temporary permission to squat in a one-room studio.

In Washington Heights, I stayed with an immigrant couple—my coworker at a restaurant and his wife who worked as a street vendor. Their two children often came home from school before their mother and always before Manuel. At the restaurant, I snuck servings of focaccia bread beneath my coat to share with my new family. Manuel snuck home whole chickens or slabs of beef. At night, I helped the children with their homework or wrestled with them on the stained carpets. Manuel would tell me about his childhood in the Dominican, about his rare trips back. He said he wanted to see the rest of the United States. But he didn't have the money.

For months my motorcycle went nowhere. It hid in an anonymous corner of that Queens garage.

It needed gas in its tank and a highway under its wheels. It needed hands on its bars that knew where they were going. The motorcycle lived off occasional oil changes and rogue mechanics' tricks learned the hard way.

I read motorcycle manuals. I scoured over maps. I

studied explorers and the paths they had forged.

When I wasn't working, I spent my time observing people, taking notes, attempting to better understand humanity and this nation. I read books about travel, about survival, about history. I spent spare evenings attending free community theatre, listening to monologues at open mic shows.

I knew I was getting ready for something. I wasn't sure what.

I saved my money. I prepared my gear. I replaced the motorcycle's worn rear tire. I searched the city for a replacement left mirror, but the motorcycle was old, bought secondhand at a budget price. I couldn't find the mirror anywhere.

The saddlebags, I re-stitched. The taillights, I replaced. The brakes, I tightened.

As much as it could be, the motorcycle was ready for departure. It waited only on me.

Chapter Five

The boy didn't know why the train had stalled. The men in the boxcar were growing restless. Their train stood at a dead stop inside a tunnel. Everyone agreed that it was too risky to get off inside the narrow passage.

The mood was tense. A couple of the men slept while others argued, shoving and shouting in the dark.

While the men were distracted, the boy made his way to a pile of luggage where he'd last seen a bag of bread. He dug through the duffels until he felt the soft plastic in his palm. He untied the twisty, slid his hand inside, pulled out one slice for himself and slipped another to the brown-skinned man sitting silently nearby.

"Gracias," whispered the Mexican.

One of the men heard the exchange. He turned to see the boy—just a diminutive silhouette in the shadows—holding the bread bag, the immigrant holding the food.

"Hey, he's takin' our bread!" the man screamed.

A second man rushed toward the boy. "I've seen him squirellin' off with it before."

A third man jumped in. "He was givin' slices away the other day. Gave it to that same new guy who hopped in from the last town."

Others agreed.

"That one that don't even speak English. Came on with nothin'. Kid gave him our bread."

One of the men grabbed the immigrant in a headlock. Others rushed toward the boy.

"We could run out of food. We might die in here because of you."

The boy stepped back, his heels hitting the wall. The boy looked around frantically in the darkness.

One of the men grabbed a glass liquor bottle. He stood over the boy, the bottle gripped tightly and held like a weapon, ready to strike. The boy was cornered.

My torso shook as the glass door slammed into my ribs, its metal handle pressing against the wad of cash in my coat pocket. I held the door open with my body and shoved my caterer's cart into the building.

I carried my entire bankroll in that jacket, planning to leave immediately following the day's work. After months of jobs, I'd squirreled away over two thousand dollars and I was one payday short of my getaway. A drop of sweat ran down my brow as I wheeled my cart toward the skyscraper's elevators.

A security guard—a white man in his thirties dressed in a worn blue suit, frayed cuffs and seem-stretched shoulders—stopped me as I approached the elevator.

"Catering lunch for Aldridge and Harris on 67," I said.

"Wait in the corner." He pointed to a bench against the glass wall, sectioned off by a red rope.

A pasty-skinned deliveryman with a pencil-thin mustache sat waiting with a load of packages on his lap.

"Damn corporate office buildings," he grunted. "Like they think they're the targets of an air raid!"

A bead of sweat ran down my forehead. The man looked at me suspiciously. I removed my jacket, opened my hand truck and shoved the coat inside.

"Been in delivery long?"

"No." I didn't even look at him, watching instead the security guard.

"What do you do then?"

"I'm leaving tonight. Heading back south."

"Oh. Oh." The man reached into his pocket, fumbled through his wallet and handed me a business card. "This is my cousin's business. They do deliveries. New Orleans." He pronounced it Or-*leans*. "They always need people."

"I'm not planning on going back that way." I extended my arm to hand back the card.

"No. No. Keep it."

Unwillingly, I slipped it into my pants pocket.

The security man lowered the phone from his ear, looked at me then nodded. He hung up.

"Okay, over here."

The pasty-skinned man stepped forward.

"Not you," said the guard. The pasty-skinned man retreated.

I walked to the guard. He ran a plastic wand over my outstretched arms and legs. It beeped as it passed my belt buckle.

I walked back to my handcart and pushed it toward the elevator.

"Hold on!" Called the guard. "Not the whole thing." He grabbed the pushcart from my hands and opened the lid. "Just the delivery."

I loaded the plastic lunch containers into my arms, balancing a dozen sandwiches and bags of chips against my chest. A bead of sweat dripped from my chin. The guard pushed the cart next to the building's main entrance.

He escorted me into the elevator and pressed the number 67. Someone called him and he slid out between the doors before they closed and disappeared already around the corner. I ascended to make the delivery.

When I returned to the lobby the security guard was nowhere to be found. My cart had vanished, and my coat and all my money inside it.

Chapter Six

With another job came another opportunity to re-build my bankroll. This time I worked in sales.

I stood on the front step of a large house with a green front door. Its brass knocker reverberated above a chipped white crack. I could hear footsteps approaching—heavy, boots maybe.

I felt someone peering out at me.

Across the street, the pitch of a fellow salesman awaited the twist of a doorknob. Up the road another half dozen of us hawked the same product. We knocked on a door. We displayed color photos of starving Asiatic villages. We coupled them with blue and red pie charts. We explained how easy it was to help with just a dollar a day.

We were in New Rochelle. Flushing, the day before. Yonkers, the day before that. Each day, they picked us up in a van at the corner of Houston and Bowery. They returned us there every night.

Per day, we were paid sixty-four dollars, twice that if we made two sales and thrice that if we made four. Failure to sell on two consecutive days resulted in immediate dismissal.

I had sold two sponsorships on my first day. Since

then, I'd scraped-by, averaging just one a day. But in Yonkers I sold none. And in Flushing I failed again. Only by begging, pleading, and telling my long and strange tale was I granted the unusual reprieve and allowed one final chance to keep my job.

"One more shot," my boss had offered. But he made me come to the office in the morning and work the phones for free.

Sitting in a cubicle, I punched a finger to the auto-dialer as I eyed the boss over my shoulder.

"Hello sir! ...yes, this is a sales call, *but...* "

My boss interjected as I moved ahead to the next call, "No, no, no, no!"

He ran his fingers through his neatly combed hair. "Handle the objection! How many times do I need to tell you? Handle the objection. Hit your pitch. Next call. Go. Make the next call."

The boss drilled me until I made a sale then sent me back out with the door-to-door team.

From the narrow window of the green door, I saw something move inside the house. I swallowed hard, my entire sales routine running through my head. The 30-second period when people will remain polite to strangers at their door begins as soon as they turn the knob.

A woman appeared in the door in front of me— heavyset, Hispanic, her hair tucked beneath a bandana. I started the pitch. "We're in your neighborhood today signing people up to sponsor children in problem areas of the world. I'm sure you've heard of dollar-a-day sponsorship programs like Feed the Children?"

I didn't wait for her response.

"Well, this is an organization just like that, and we're working hard to bring healthcare and education to the millions of people all over the world who are dying of curable diseases."

I flipped open my notebook, moving fast not to lose her attention.

"This is Tushina," I said, pointing to a four-by-six glossy photo I'd slid into my binder cover. "She's my adopted friend. As her sponsor, she sends me a photo of herself every month along with a letter about how she and her village are progressing."

The woman stared at the photo, her brown forehead wrinkling with thought.

"Sometimes Tushina even mails me hand-drawn pictures from the school that I help fund for her."

Had I called her Tunisha?

Had I said she lived just outside of India? Or could I talk about her parents slaving away in the Sierra Leone diamond mines?

The woman shook her head. "I speak... little English," she said. "I only housekeeper," she giggled, her belly shaking a little as she showed me the mop in one hand.

She hadn't taken her brown eyes off of the girl's photo—the poor, wiry-haired little thing sitting on a dirt stool, barefoot. The tents of some desperate, fly-ridden village lay in the background.

"How much?" asked the housekeeper, walking a few steps to the back of the foyer and grabbing a purse.

The checkbook was flying out of her bag. The pen was scribbling, the paper tearing, the money sailing into the air and halfway across the world from one poor person to another, making a stop in between where I deducted my sixty-four dollar cut, another stop for the company executives to deduct their fees, probably detouring to countless other destinations, picked apart a dollar at a time before it reached whatever child in whichever remote hell of the earth.

The green door closed in front of me, and I just stood there: my notebook in one hand, her check in the other, a blank stare on my face.

A car horn jolted me. It was our van waiting to leave for Manhattan. I had earned another day of employment.

By Friday's end, however, after another two-day sales drought, I was looking for another job.

Before long, I was working in the kitchen of an Italian restaurant—an expensive joint with a high-class façade and low-budget innards. The broken dishwasher rumbled like a cement mixer. The hot-water function hadn't worked in months. We served food on plates scrubbed with soap and cold water. I sometimes used my fingernails to scratch off dried specks of food. We all knew better than to bring it up with management.

In the back room, Manuel filled the Grey Goose bottles with discount vodka. Roberto set mousetraps in the pantry. The hostess did her little dance with the customers: "We bake all of our own bread, and our dessert chef makes a wonderful tiramisu from scratch." She referred to the supply closet by a much grander name: "Let me call back and see if we have that year in the wine cellar."

In the kitchen, a crew of Hispanic workers

defrosted dinner rolls and microwaved amaretto cake. Our chef, an older white man, prepared the lamb sauce, shouting at his staff in broken Spanish. Except for him, we all worked under the table, paid in cash every Friday.

The waiters rumored that our weekly pay was laundered money from a more lucrative enterprise— insurance fraud, or union racketeering, or the black market clothing industry. The owner, Dominique, was a sharply dressed middle-aged man with slicked-back white hair. Both Manuel and Roberto repeatedly whispered to me that he was well connected in the organized crime ring. They'd worked for him at a nightclub years earlier. The place had gone bust after a raid by federal agents, and Dominique had served two years in prison for tax evasion.

More rumors circulated among the Spanish-speaking staff. Dom, they said, had gotten in way over his head with the restaurant, and some mafia types had forced him to go partners with Anthony, our boss. Anthony, they said, was an enforcer for a kingpin and knee-deep in the narcotics trade. He could do anything he wanted and no one could stop him.

But these were only rumors, there was never anything to act on, just speculations that reinforced the notion that we were stuck between poverty and crime.

Dom spent most of his time in his office in the basement, and we knew well enough to stay away. Anthony spent a lot of time down there too, often accompanying strangers in flashy suits.

Anthony would sometimes return with scrapes on his arms or with skin missing from his knuckles, walking up the kitchen steps with his sport coat removed, his tie loosened, sweat soaking through his shirt. He would throw trays of silverware or yell at the employees, his deep voice and Brooklyn accent resonating throughout the metallic kitchen, his burley frame lumbering across the rubber floor mats.

This was one of those days.

"What the hell are you doing standing around?" Anthony shouted. He punched the aluminum countertop.

I was waiting for some bread to finish in the microwave.

Anthony rubbed his nose and sniffled. He was always rubbing his nose and sniffling.

"Hurry it up!" He slammed the counter again.

He moved toward the register and began shuffling through our receipts. Dom's voice called him from the basement, and he walked back downstairs.

I took the bread into the dining room then returned to polish the champagne glasses covered in dust. I exhaled on them and rubbed the mist off with a dishrag. I loaded the glasses onto trays and carried them into the ballroom.

A jazz band was setting up as I walked through the double doors, the guitarist fingering a few chords. Manuel was rolling tables into place. I carried the trays over each shoulder just as he had trained me.

A week earlier, Anthony had hired a fourth man to do our job. We couldn't afford to lose any hours or split any tips, so we'd sabotaged his shifts. Manuel hid most of the glasses in a back closet. Roberto and I hid plates and silverware. We stashed everything we could, gave only the most vague answers to his questions, and watched him fumble around the kitchen until he was fired.

I was picking up the second load of champagne glasses in the kitchen when I heard Anthony's heavy feet booming up the stairs. I hurried. I was almost out the door.

"Hey," Anthony said. His voice shook me, the tray of glasses unsteady in my hand. "Here." He reached out his right hand, a fold of green bills in it. I had almost forgotten it was Friday.

"Thank you," I said. He walked away as I flipped the bills between my thumb and index fingers, trying to count them with my one free hand. I grunted as I noticed the stack was at least a hundred short. Anthony heard me and turned. He looked into my eyes, calmly, menacingly.

"Is there a problem," he said. His accent was sharp and without the intonation of a question mark.

I shook my head.

On the subway, I saw a man in a wheelchair with a thick beard stained with food droppings. He wore several sweaters, all of them torn and brown with muck. Steam came from his mouth. I wondered if I'd end up this way—beaten and friendless. He rolled himself down the platform, through a gate and down a causeway.

I walked to the west exit of the station, then down 168th street toward Manuel's shoebox apartment. The crisp evening, lit with headlights and street-lamps, was soundtracked with car horns and buzzing tires on trafficked streets. I left my boots on the torn rug by the door. Inside, the room was warm and quiet.

His daughter was crying when I entered. His son colored in a book with a red crayon.

I pulled a loaf of focaccia bread from my coat and left it on the table. The two kids rose to join me in the kitchen. The girl leaned on the fridge. I opened two boxes of macaroni and began dinner. No one else would be back for at least an hour.

When Manuel and his wife returned, the evening glowed with familial warmth. I reclined on a tattered yellow sofa in the living room. The kids watched television from the floor while Manuel, in an easy chair, read aloud the tabloid headlines of the *New York Post*. His wife, in the kitchen, scooped up some sort of cream-based desert.

I'd been waiting several days to talk to Manuel. Once everyone else had gone to bed, I told him how Anthony had shorted me for the second time in two weeks.

It had happened to him too.

"The whole kitchen," he said. "We're afraid."

The kitchen staff was afraid Anthony would call immigration if they complained. Manuel told me he'd been looking for another job, but begged me not to go to the authorities. I promised I wouldn't.

At the restaurant the next day, I waited for a good opportunity. At the bottom of the kitchen stairs, overflowing carts of dirty linens lined the hallway. I tiptoed across the shadowy corridor, creaked open the office door. Anthony had left, and Dom was busy.

I entered the dark room. A baby grand piano sat

beneath a layer of dust. Upholstered armchairs, stacked three-high, lined the walls. In a corner were two oversized desks. I heard something by the door and paused. My heart was nearly beating out of my chest, but I didn't hear the sound again.

Looking through Anthony's desk, I found nothing, just some logbooks. His drawers held rows of files. In his chair was a pack of cigarettes, a box of pens, and a can of cat food—who knew what that was for.

In the corner, against the brick wall I found two shoeboxes and opened the first.

Cash. Stacked and rubber-banded. All in ones. Three hundred maybe. I needed more though. It needed to be enough to share with the kitchen staff. I opened the second box.

White powder wrapped in plastic. Each baggie was twisted off in a little ball and tied with a rubber band.

Footsteps creaked down the stairs. I stood, shifting my head shoulder-to-shoulder, looking for a place to hide. The footsteps quickened.

I ducked behind a small sofa. Even on my knees, I towered over it. Too small. I stood up. It was useless. There was nowhere to hide.

The footsteps stopped. The light turned on, flickered for a moment. Anthony saw me, and calmly pulled the door closed behind him, leaving it an inch ajar. A draft sent chill bumps up my spine.

Anthony moved toward me. He didn't know I'd lied on my job application. He didn't know I was about to steal from him. He just knew I was someplace I never should have been.

"What are you doing down here? What were you

lookin' to take?" His words weren't so much questions as they were taunts. "Are you lying now?" He brought his face closer and closer to mine.

Anthony punched me to the ground. The overhead light sputtered. He lifted me up and held me against the wall by the neck. The bulb flickered off. A luminous beam from the doorway struck my face like a spotlight. I stared into the blinding white blur.

With his back to the wall of the boxcar, the boy looked at the shadowed faces of his adversaries. Standing in the darkness of the corner, he saw a shred of light from the open doorway.

Furiously the boy elbowed his way between the men. One of them grabbed hold of his arm. The boy was thrown to the ground. He was kicked. He was spat on. He felt a cut on his head.

The train lurched forward, beginning to move again. The boy crawled to his feet and sprinted out the door, falling to the tunnel's coal-black ballast as the train began to accelerate.

The boy scrambled to his feet. He ran as fast as he could after the train. He saw the steel ladder at the rear of the last car, the steps leading up to the unoccupied roof.

He lunged for it.

I was sprinting across Midtown, blood dripping down my face and one of the city's most dangerous mobsters on my tail. I must've fought my way out of the restaurant basement. **I must've taken some pretty ferocious blows, too.** I hurdled a subway turnstile and raced across the station after a departing train.

By the time I was within spitting distance, the doors had closed and the cars were already gaining speed. But the handles at the rear of the train were just inches from my reach. I took two more hard strides and leaped from the subway platform toward the car. My hands clenched the steel grips, and I swung my feet onto the ledge of the closed doorway. I held on tightly. The train zoomed through the dark tunnel.

I was leaving New York City, and I was leaving fast.

Chapter Seven

The audience is silent. I stare out at them for what seems like an eternity. The memories are fuzzy, some parts too confusing, too ridiculous even for me to accept, but I've told it anyway. Right or wrong, I've said everything just as it reappears in my memory.

I struggle to remember the rest. What happened after New York City? How did I get started in show business? Where did I run to? Which parts are true?

A flash of images sprints through my mind. The labrador pawing at my apartment door, whining as she rubs her snout against the wood. The landlord looks up from his pruning sheers. He walks across the parking lot and stops at the door, taking the torn sheet of notebook paper from the doorknob. He looks at my message and twists the knob. He peaks inside. The dog follows him in. The dishes are piled in the sink, clothes and papers strewn about the floor.

"He left! Well whattaya know."

The next image is bright in my mind.

Inside a farmhouse, the father of the runaway boy steps over a stack of baseball cards. He sits down at a desk, beside his son's unmade bed. The boy's catcher's mitt sits on an overhead shelf. The man stares out the window at walnut trees and the John Deere. He gazes through the branches at the railroad tracks. A train whistles in the distance.

A woman in the audience snickers. I try to focus. I need to say something.

I picture the beautiful blonde in her dorm room. She slips a few sheets of paper from a drawer, and begins to write, tears streaming down her cheek. When she's finished, she reads over what she's written. From a drawer she pulls out a framed photograph of herself with a young man.

A knock on the door snaps her away from his greenish eyes.

"You ready to go?" a different man says.

She slips the photograph back into its place.

"Just a sec."

She folds the letter into an envelope and licks the seal. She rubs the tears from her eyes.

"I'm ready."

She grabs her purse, takes hold of the man's hand and walks out the door.

I look out to the crowd, but all I see is the blinding spotlight. The pain must be obvious on my face. The audience begins to murmur.

I take a deep breath and I let the heartbreak linger.

Then, I wipe my brow and resume the story.

If a mobster had been chasing me, I must've lost him on the subway. No one had trailed me through Queens, and no one had followed me into the garage where my motorcycle sat waiting.

I strapped my bags to the bike and fired it up. I headed straight out of town, the winter wind biting the bloody scrapes on my face.

On the Triborough Bridge, I fumbled for my wallet hoping the attendant would just raise the mechanical arm and wave me through. I had actually put the kickstand down and was feigning to search for change in my saddlebags, two miles of cars honking behind me, when the woman in the tollbooth finally gave-in. I pulled the same stunt on the George Washington. I had only about three hundred dollars and I couldn't afford to lose any of them on tolls.

Through the glass of my motorcycle's remaining rearview, I saw the lights of New York City, a glowing goliath receding in the distance. I survived the beast, but I would have to endure the brutal winter until I reached the southern climate.

I shivered. My fingers went numb on the handlebars. In my rearview, New York City faded as quickly as my memory.

How had I gotten my backpacks? What happened to Manuel? Where had I woken up the previous morning? What did I wear? I don't remember.

I can see clearly the image of the first truck stop a few miles south on I-95, glowing neon red in the night. Inside, its floor was freshly mopped. Newspaper headlines told of an escalating war, about our troops being sent into treacherous mountains to haul militants out of caves, about a conflict in the desert. I can see those headlines exactly as they were.

The cashier kept his eye on me as I walked around

61

the store with dried blood on my face, my cheeks
swollen nearly over my eyes.

Ducking into an aisle out of view, I emptied my
pockets onto a shelf: some pocket lint; a fistful of
receipts; three hundred dollars in cash, all rolled in a
rubber-band; and a business card for a delivery
company in New Orleans.

A bus ticket would be the cheapest mode of travel.
For a hundred and ten dollars, I could ride nearly
anywhere—even a seventy-three hour ride to California
that included five transfers and nearly four dozen stops
through dusty Midwestern towns.

But unwilling to part with the motorcycle, I had no
choice but to fight sub-freezing temperatures until I
made it into the south.

Stepping outside again, back into the cold, I
enviously watched Greyhound passengers standing on
the curb as they waited to re-board. A Latino kid spoke
Spanish in a near whisper into a telephone. A crying
baby held tightly to its mother's neck. An obese man in
a blue sweat-suit licked his orange fingers before
dipping them back into his bag of Cheetos.

A tattooed woman with circles beneath both eyes
as dark as bruises scratched her forearms and twitched
manically. A black man—called "Shorty" by a heavy
mother and son pair standing behind him—wore a high
collared leather jacket. A bearded man carried a bible
and two cardboard signs protesting the government.

"DC bound," I heard him say.

One of the passengers, a lady destined for some
Florida town where she hoped to redirect a life of
abusive boyfriends and minimum wage jobs, said that

she'd stuffed everything she owned in two black trash bags.

When the bus arrived, all of these people walked forward and boarded. The bus grunted toward the highway's on-ramp and disappeared out of sight.

Back inside, I unfolded the map I'd bought and traced my fingers over the Jersey Turnpike. With the tip of a dried-out pen, I scratched out several routes, staying clear of the overcrowded interstate highways.

The cold wind howled on the convenience store's window. My shivering body begged me to leave the motorcycle behind.

I saw myself as if in a dream, hitchhiking on the I-495 on-ramp, snow collecting on my shoulders as I walked backward in the headlights of oncoming cars.

Who would those drivers think I was? Would they trust me or would they question me about my past?

"How long you been on the road? What were you doing in New York City? What are ya settin' out to do now?"

A man at the truck stop watched me, and he peered out toward the highway to see what I was looking at.

"You alright son?"

"Just warming up," I said.

I pulled the business card from my pocket and looked at the New Orleans address. Putting on my gloves, I walked back out to the motorcycle.

Staying clear of the massive Interstates, I followed what seemed like an endless rural highway, driving against wind and sleet. When darkness came, I pulled over and made camp in the snow beside the road. I was willing to sleep anywhere.

I woke up well before dawn shivering in the pitch-blackness and couldn't fall back asleep. It was a windless morning, and the pencil-thin branches of tall oaks balanced stacks of snow. The chill burned my eyes and tears streamed down my cheeks. I regretted having spent the night outside. Now, as I tried to put the motorcycle back on the road, I was paying an additional price. I dropped to my knees and dug with bare hands at the ice that encased the lower half of the motorcycle.

No cars passed. No birds flew over the snow-driven pastures. No chimney smoked from the lone house on the horizon. No dogs barked.

My fingers went numb. The deadening sensation grew up my arms until it seemed they were no longer a part of me. My knees lost feeling. Then my legs. My stomach and chest followed. I surrendered to the snowy ground, and numbness spread inside my ribs, overtaking my lungs, overwhelming my heart. I could feel only the inside of my skull as my thoughts began to escape down southbound roads.

I was the breeze against my ears. I was the snowflake carried across the land. I was the sun sliding across the sky.

I was the stranded explorer, trekking across snowy mountains toward refuge. I was the lone scout dependent on my sure-footed steed. I was the earth-colored native chased from my settlement, hiding in the cold hills.

I was Neanderthal building fire to keep from freezing. I was the outlaw heating my fugitive hands above the flames. I was a trailblazer. I was Daniel

Boone leading a pick-ax team through the Cumberland Gap. I was the patriot running supply lines from the freezing north to ambush the Brits in sunny Charleston. I was the obedient soldier indifferent to circumstance.

Miserably, wearily, I was alive.

The snow beneath his sleeping bag began to melt. The soldier scooted to the other side of his green canvas tent. With a gloved hand, he pulled aside the tent flaps and peeked out. Snow poured down.

The young soldier from Arkansas had been sent here for his first deployment, to this remote mountain camp where he did little else than walk rifle patrols. Occasionally he raided spider-holes, his M-16 at the ready and his night vision goggles over his leaf-green eyes. Most his days were spent shivering in his sleeping bag, his weapon in his hand, his thoughts wandering to his woman in her dorm room, far, far away.

Footsteps cracked the ice-covered snow. The soldier peered through his tent.

"Mail." A corporal handed him a letter.

The soldier tore it from the envelope. He suspected what it was by the return address. His throat tightened as he unfolded the pages. His fiancé's handwriting was deliberate and legible.

After he read the letter, he crumpled it into a ball and held it tightly in his fist. He blamed himself.

I became accustomed to loneliness and danger.

There was the time an icy highway almost pulled me beneath the tires of a speeding eighteen-wheeler. There was the time a blind curve on a frozen mountain pass almost swept me off a cliff. There was the time a crash into a snow ditch left me half-conscious. And there were the many nights I almost froze to death. On the coldest of them, I woke every few hours to massage the blood into my toes and toss a log on the glowing embers. Just outside Gypsy, West Virginia, freezing rain prevented me from building a fire. By sunrise, my soaked sleeping bag had frozen and my toes were blue.

Under similar conditions in Grundy, Virginia, I spent half of my remaining funds on a motel room.

Almost out of money and ill with the flu, I passed placards marking my entry to the Bible belt. Large letters on the broad side of a barn along Highway 460 read, "At the end of the road, you find what you sought." Hand painted signs nailed to trees announced, "The end is coming." Wooden stakes approaching the Cumberland Gap held large painted boards reading, "Be ready to meet your maker." Cross-emblazoned billboards repeated messages of destiny and fate.

It took me nearly two weeks to ride just 800 miles into Pineville, Kentucky—sometimes advancing as little as 30 miles a day in snowstorms. But once out of the Appalachians, it was warm enough to loosen my oilskin parka.

The next day I drove clear through Tennessee, bolted through Memphis along Highway 61, and sank into the spring sunshine of Mississippi.

Less than forty dollars remained in my pocket. Maybe it was just the pontificating road signs of the Bible Belt, and maybe it had something to do with the lure of the Mississippi River, but something told me I was supposed to drive to the end of Highway 61—all the

way to the river's mighty mouth, into the heart of New
Orleans. If I reached New Orleans, the business card
would mean lodging and labor. I just needed enough
money to continue the trip.

In a Robinsonville casino on the Mississippi Delta, I
spun a roulette wheel for middle-aged Southern
tourists—their eyes aglow with the blue neon lights that
popped and fizzled from the lounge behind me. At
another shift, I shuffled blackjack decks and slid cards
across the felt, laying another down each time a
gambler said "hit."

On the other side of Robinsonville, I lived in a
motel for a hundred dollars a week. Many of the rooms
were used as subsidized housing, and more than a few
of the tenants were drug addicts and prostitutes.

Coming home from work one night, I heard a
knock at my door. Chantell, my neighbor, the one with
pocked cheeks and meth-eaten teeth, was hopeful I
would accept a solicitation.

"Just twenty dollars?" she offered.

"You can have the money."

"God. You mean it?"

"Take it."

"Oh, thank you."

I opened the door and let her sit on the wooden
chair while I pulled the bill from my wallet. Her face
was dogged with scratch marks, her lips dry and heavy.

She once worked as a supermarket cashier, she
told me as she pulled an ashy spoon from her pocket,
thumbing its brown chemical stains.

"Make my own schedule now," she bragged. "Never

work min'm wage again. No mo'."

I didn't know what to say.

"God, I gotta get fixed." She put the spoon back in her pocket and limped to the room of another neighbor. I locked the door behind her.

The whore, the drug-pusher, the pimp—these were my peers at every weekly-rate motel. They shared a freedom from the nine-to-five. They shared an addiction.

Meanwhile, I worked shift labor along the Mississippi. Outside of Tunica, I unloaded small cargo ships. South of there, I anchored personal watercrafts at a riverfront restaurant. From town to town, I worked my way to New Orleans.

Traveling south on a moonless midnight, I headed out of Clarksdale, finally bound for New Orleans. That's when I was stopped at a fork in the road.

Two police cars barricaded the diverging highways, their red and white lights flashed under the unlit sky.

"Hands over your head!" The voice boomed through a bullhorn.

A spotlight's beam lit my hands and head.

"Keep 'em high. Turn slow."

I raised my arms and faced the policemen. They hid behind their cruisers, both doors open.

"On the ground. Lay Down. Both arms out. Now! Now!"

The road was cold against my jaw.

"Away from your chest!"

I extended my arms. Two shadows approached. Three or four more officers stood in the distance.

The policeman pulled handcuffs from his belt and

clicked them around my wrists. He stood me up and ducked me into the squad car.

"What's this all about?" I pleaded.

The officer slammed the door.

Chapter Eight

Days later, I was resting beneath an awning at a gas station in northern Louisiana and saw an ambiguous police bulletin that must have been related to my arrest: *WANTED—white male, early twenties, green or brown eyes, blonde or brown hair; last seen on motorcycle in western Mississippi, could be traveling by industrial rail; possibly former military; consider highly dangerous.*

Maybe my look-alike was wanted for fraud. Maybe he'd absconded with the church funds and ran off with the preacher's daughter, or maybe he'd killed a man in a crime of passion.

My jailers released me in less than twenty-four hours, saying they could hold me no longer without formal charges even though, as the deputy said, a guy like me "shouldn't be allowed to go around looking so suspicious, not when people from all over the world are trying to blow our country apart and attack our freedom."

The police department offered no apologies. They warned me not to return.

There was nothing I could do except travel on. So I

drove into the swamps of Louisiana, watching the sunset reflected red on stagnant waterways and the hairline stems of green plants hiding alligators.

Highway 61 merged into a maze of overpasses and interchanges circling New Orleans. As I exited, I passed the globular Superdome. Moments later, I watched the throngs of drunken college students in the French Quarter. I drove past two blocks of freshly painted restaurants and shiny new hotels, then past mile after mile of dilapidated buildings and homes. A grimy brown line beneath second-story windows told the tale of floodwater and its victims. The streets were deserted.

The business card proved useless. There was no longer anyone at the address. The building was abandoned. The phone number was disconnected. A recent hurricane had destroyed that section of town.

I drove back toward the French Quarter then wandered into an all-night saloon on Bourbon Street. I met a thin construction worker on a bender. He was dressed in cowboy garb—straw hat, boots, and a blue-green checkered shirt with pearl snaps. He said he had some work I could do for him the next day, and he let me sleep in the back of his pickup truck parked outside.

I woke at sunrise, wrapped up in a blue tarp in the bed of the man's pickup. I wasted the day waiting for him, but he never returned to the vehicle, so I slept in the back of his truck for a second night.

On the morning of day three, I spent the last of my money on a bagel and a cup of coffee.

"You know sweetheart," the brunette waitress said from the other side of the counter, "you could just turn around and go back wherever you came from."

I took a bite from the bagel.

"There ain't no work here anymore," she said. "The city's lucky anyone even showed up for Mardi Gras."

I sipped from the mug.

"The storm took everything, hun." She paused. "The only people making money in this town are hotel owners and guys slinging drinks on Bourbon Street. And trust me, those jobs are taken. There ain't even places to live anymore."

I thanked her for her concern and walked away, leaving my bagel half-eaten and my coffee half-full.

With a quarter tank of gas remaining in the motorcycle, I set across New Orleans searching for any opportunity. I passed the abandoned housing projects and the flood-ridden shacks, drove over the rusted trolley tracks of Desire Street, and entered the wasteland that had become the Ninth Ward. To do so, I traversed mud-washed streets so pocked with four-foot pot holes that I often had to re-route, turning around to navigate the narrow wheels of the motorcycle through less treacherous cross-streets. I was four miles from the well-funded bars on Bourbon Street and the expensive storefronts in the French Quarter, but I may well have been in another nation entirely.

Tall weeds grew from fields of refuse and framed the concrete slabs where homes once stood. Against telephone poles where the high-water mark was easily fifteen feet high, the smashed skeletons of houses sat like broken bumper cars piled into a corner. The levy had provided a barricade upon which washed-away homes had been swept.

I turned eastward again. From the upper Ninth

Ward, I headed into the district's lower section and passed more flood-ridden shacks until I eventually came upon a three-story brick building with a sign on its front reading "St Mary's School." It was impossible to miss. For one thing, it was one of the only buildings still standing. For another, its yard was full of dreadlocked and tattooed twenty-somethings, white and black, picking garbage from an adjacent field. On the cracked sidewalk, shirtless black children rode rusted bicycles. An old school bus—its yellow exterior painted over with multi-color flowers and handprints—sat with its engine running and its rear door ajar. A rag-tag crew of workers piled out of the vehicle.

I don't know what story I told them when I introduced myself, but they paid no much attention to it.

"Grab that crate of Tyvek suits, will you?" said a gray-haired hippy.

I carried the crate up the front steps and into what looked to be the lobby of a high school circa 1950. The place was a mess, with orange extension cords crisscrossing its cratered tile floor. It looked like it had survived a bombing.

In an adjacent large-windowed room that looked to have once been the attendance office, sleeping bags and crates of apples—flies buzzing about them—sat on waterlogged floorboards. The carpeting had been torn away leaving only rotten, warped wooden flooring.

"Got contaminated with black mold," said a girl with a nose ring when she caught me staring at the floor.

I asked her about staying there, and she motioned

me to follow her upstairs. The mess of curly hair on her head seemed to contain the subtle hint of marijuana odor. The bottoms of her bare feet were black as soot.

Upstairs was the library. Books were scattered about the room and piled around cots and sleeping bags. More cots filled the classrooms and the teachers' lounge. Poems and pictures, etched in chalk, filled the blackboards. Yellow caution tape roped off the bathrooms and water fountains.

On the third story, more tents and sleeping bags covered classrooms. A large window opened to a flat roof covered by several tents. Desks had been moved to make way for people climbing in and out through the sliding glass panes. Along the other walls, desks piled almost to the ceiling.

When the hurricane had hit, people seeking shelter had been trapped inside the school. After the levy broke, they stacked the desks to provide higher ground, fearing the rising waters. An old women died in a now closed off third story room. It had been days before helicopters and boats came and her body could be taken away.

The underfunded school, which already was past due for a renovation, had become the only shelter in the neighborhood during the storm, and the only rally point for community members afterward. About a hundred people (half volunteers, half local refugees) were actually living there. Now I'd be joining them.

From behind a bookcase, two pre-adolescent boys, their black skin dry and ashy, jumped out and screamed with laughter. They pushed between us and scampered down the stairs. A white man, three silver hoops dangling from each ear, laughed and chased after them.

"I'm coming for you," he said.

"Hide-and-seek," the girl with the nose ring explained preemptively.

She turned down the stairs. "This place look alright?"

It was nothing permanent, just a bastion for people who were waiting—waiting for help, waiting for fortunes to change, waiting for an opportunity.

"Count me in," I nodded.

"Good," she said. "Work starts at seven tomorrow."

I spent the next day shoveling mold and mud into a wheelbarrow. My gas mask hugged tightly to my cheekbones and the vacuum-like roar of my breaths rang in my ears.

With snow shovels we dug out the carpeting and floors. With pick axes we ripped down the dilapidated walls. We were deconstructing the house to its skeleton so maybe eventually someone else would reconstruct it, with bright new paint on the walls and soft carpeting in every hallway. First we needed to excavate the hurricane sludge.

Through the fog of my mask, I squinted at other volunteers pulling something from beneath a mold-ridden couch.

Outside, we wiped broken drywall from the sleeves of our suits and removed our goggles and gloves. We sat on the tailgate of the meal truck.

Over a lunch of warm stew and old bread, I read part of a John Bunyan book that I found in the school's library. It was the story of a man who abandons his home and family. It never explains why.

The other volunteers dug into their food and passed around the things they'd found while gutting the house.

"You can still make out most of these photos," Steven said, handing me a water-stained album they discovered under the sofa.

In one photo, a black boy with puffed cheeks blew at eight candles on a cake. In another photo, a family of four stood proudly in front of an old sedan—the price from the used-car lot still painted in pink and yellow on the windshield.

After lunch we geared up again. We re-entered the house, dragged away the furniture and carpets, dug our pick axes into the drywall, tore the house from its frame as best we could, and retreated to our shelter for the night. The next day, at another house, we did it all over again.

There was more work than gutting houses. We had childcare. We had a women's center. We had a team of gardeners and farmers, a construction crew, kitchen workers, countless organizational positions, and even a real doctor and nurse team. We ran a shelter for displaced families. Then there were two or three people in charge of accumulating grant money.

At one time or another, I was everyone in the organization: the house gutter, the gardener, the photographer, the cook, the shelter manager, the grant writer, and the refugee. Neither inexperience nor ineptitude was an excuse for inaction. We all did what we could. And what we couldn't do, we at least tried.

The locals were undereducated graduates and

dropouts of poorly funded public schools in high-crime neighborhoods. These people were resourceful, full of action, and quickly angered when their hopes went unfulfilled. As unpaid volunteers, we were their heroes when things went well, their scapegoats when things went poorly.

Some of the volunteers were upper-middle-class white kids who dropped out of college. Others had left home at an earlier age. A few had dropped out of high school. Some of them, like the hurricane refugees themselves, had come here with nowhere else to go.

It was that strange combination of chance and choice that landed us all here. The locals sometimes chastised the volunteers, who they saw as carpetbaggers. Why had they come to New Orleans to live amongst the poorest in the nation? Some of the locals were insulted and felt that the goals they'd been taught to strive for were being disregarded or rejected. If the rich must live as the poor to attain happiness, what then were the poor to do?

We were white and we were black. We were angry old women and disaffected teenage boys. We were refugees from a storm—both a cataclysmic display of nature's indifference and a mind-blowing exhibit of our own inner-conflicts.

Volunteers and locals alike broke down in temper tantrums. Once, I watched two volunteers break into a fistfight while gutting a house. Several times, mostly after drunken Saturday nights, arguments raged throughout our makeshift dormitory.

Later, when I served as the live-in manager of the family shelter, arguments erupted nightly as all the tenants returned from retrieving their children from school. One evening, I stepped into the kitchen and found Tina crying over the sink.

"Someone better keep that girl Lindsey in check! You hear me?" she shouted. Tina splashed her fist into the soapy water as she continued with the dishes. Tears poured down her brown cheeks. Dirty dishwater splashed on the linoleum floor. "I'm a forty-nine year old woman. I don't need a twenty-one year old white girl to tell me to clean up after myself."

I nodded. I noticed Regina sitting at the table across the room, looking enraged by Tina's speech.

Tina pounded her palm against the plywood of the makeshift countertop. At the table, Regina roared, "I don't know who y'all think you are. Bossin' us around, tellin' us to clean-up after ourselves, tellin' us to watch *our* kids." The residents of the family shelter were converging on me.

From the hall I heard Randy's shouts nearing. "Something's got to be done! We was fine before y'all came in here with rules. Y'all get all nosy and getting' up in our business!"

Behind Randy was Jermichael.

I gathered that Lindsey had just been run-out by Tina after a fight over the household chores right before I stepped into the scene.

The residents rallied. Their anger—founded in collective uncertainty—was brewing.

For a moment I stood against the swirling gusts of their fury and assessed the situation. I looked Tina in the eye, reached an arm over her shoulder and invited to walk with me outside.

A few steps from the door she broke down. The homelessness, the joblessness, the crowded one bedroom house filled with twelve messy people... she was on edge.

I hugged her and her wet face dripped on the shoulder of my t-shirt. As we walked, she apologized for yelling at me. She apologized for chasing Lindsey away. She apologized for stirring the emotions of the other residents. I nodded.

I led Tina, still panting with emotion, past the ruins of our block and into the rubble of what had been a churchyard. We sat on the steps while she lit a cigarette. The final rays of sunset reflected off the few tears on her cheeks. Behind her were the piles of rubble that had once been homes. Shadowing us from the right were the remains of the St. Bernard Projects, now barb-wired shut, keeping out the tenants who once called them home.

Tina stopped crying as she puffed a gray cloud off her cigarette. In the silence, I heard Lindsey's footsteps from behind. The two embraced as they apologized to each other.

I heard a loud engine nearby and tires kicking up gravel on the next block over. As I looked up, a HUM-V appeared from around the corner and braked to a halt at the entrance to the churchyard. Two National Guardsmen slammed doors behind them and approached us as silhouettes in the headlights, M-16s held out before them, muzzles angled toward the ground.

"Stay here," I whispered to Lindsey and left her and Tina on the stoop as I walked to the soldiers with both hands open, arms extended over my head.

From feet away I read their insignia and addressed the men at rank: Sergeant and Lieutenant. They listened as I explained our trespassing—the crowded two room house we used as a shelter, the single toilet and shower, the six children and six adults who shared the cramped space, the overflow of emotion, the need for privacy.

I shook hands with both soldiers. They drove off to investigate more suspicious happenings.

Another conflict averted, our waiting place would last another day.

Running the shelter, I was a politician. Living there, I was a homeless refugee. I was part hapless freeloader and part struggling laborer. The strangers around me were my only family.

Reconstructing homes, I was a Christian on a mission trip with the sun on my neck, a tool belt around my waist.

Organizing the shelter's paperwork, I was a college student on a Spring Break trip with my Social Work class.

I was a forty-seven year old single mother fixing the greasy chain on her son's bike. I was a dropout of a segregated school system. I was the daughter of parents raised in the Jim Crow South.

I was a National Guardsman, just home from one war and assigned to assist the New Orleans Police Department with another. I combed the streets, watching drug-dealers exchange payments and merchandise.

Walking down the abandoned, washed-out

alleyways of New Orleans' infamous Florida Projects, I was a suspect to cops who interrogated me about narcotics trades and concealed weapons.

I had good friends there. The residents at the shelter had become my family. It seemed ironically serene, even though I knew I was tired and frustrated and the world around me looked irreparably damaged. Well meaning, hard working, open minded, and desperately poor, I was among the self-appointed handlers of a national emergency—the restorers of homes, the daycare providers for single parents, the ones who adopted those who were lost.

The lobby at New Orleans's Social Services office was a windowless room at the back of a two-story office building, well hidden beneath the high-rise towers on Poydras Street. There were no signs for the place. The listing in the phone book provided a disconnected number and a former address. It took me all afternoon to find it. When I finally got there, I found it empty and sat alone in a thinly upholstered chair. After a long wait, a slender white woman came to the counter and directed me back to her cubicle. Soft rock played on a radio on a nearby desk. Her brown hair fell in her eyes as she looked at the paperwork I handed her.

"Picking up a single-parent childcare subsidy form?" she confirmed.

"Yes."

She looked again at the stapled sheets of paper.

"I need the proof of employment."

I handed her the pay stub.

She read it aloud. "Rodney Harrison, Beaux

Brothers Construction Company."

"It's *Randy*."

She looked again at the pay stub and typed something into her computer, placing the stub on a stack by her phone. "Can I see your ID, Mr. Harrison?"

"I'm not Mr. Harrison," I explained. "He's at work."

She paused and looked up from the paperwork. "Well, he needs to do this in person."

"I can bring him the paperwork," I said. "I manage the shelter where he lives."

"He needs to receive it *in person*."

"But he's at work."

"Well, he'll have to come when he's not working."

That's when I went berserk, embarrassingly so. "He works Monday through Friday. He just got the job. He can't take any time off to come here, and he couldn't afford to lose those hours even if he were allowed to."

"That's the rule," she said. She pointed to the small print on the form and recited it: "The person applying for services must appear *in person*, anytime between nine and five Monday through Friday."

"This is absurd," I interrupted.

"Sir," she said with some comfort in her voice. "It's not absurd, sir. It's how the system works."

"But he can't come to the office. Nine to five. That's when he *works*. That's when *everybody* works." I stood up from the chair. It was all I could do not to throw it. "He came down here to do this before he started working. But he couldn't get the forms," I yelled in her face. "And do you know why?" I asked. "Do you know why?"

She was speechless.

"Because you can't get the application without *proof* of employment."

The woman had gotten to her feet. She was pointing an extended finger at me. "Tell Mr. Harrison he'll have to *find* a way."

The next day, I had a similar experience at the transportation office. The man behind the counter spoke as though from a script.

"The city council has decided to stop running buses to that part of town," he said. "Those people will just have to drive across town to work."

"*Those people* can't afford cars!" I argued, but got no response.

Angrily, I walked down the stairs and out onto the humid street.

Back at the shelter, the federal government was already demanding we return the few trailer homes they'd given us. Even with all of our hard work, we seemed always to be running out of resources.

While some of the housemates at the shelter had acquired jobs and moved into leased apartments, thousands of others across New Orleans were unable to make ends meet. Every day, more people showed up at the shelter. Our funding was of greater and greater concern, not only to those who had administrated the house to begin with, but also to the residents who had assumed larger roles in running the house. To make matters even more complex, our group was evolving into some other kind of community-slash-political action committee, one with extreme leanings.

Rumor had it that some of the residents wanted to use tactics they'd used as Black Panthers in the '70s.

There were other strong voices that advocated anarchy and spoke of local police and government as our enemies in war. Years later, I would read in a newspaper about one of my fellow volunteers acting as an FBI informant. Internal divisions were being formed, and I began hearing word that coups were being planned. A power struggle was on.

It was a good time for me to leave.

Chapter Nine

I lay belly-up in the darkness of some untilled acreage, my sleeping bag stretched out in an open field. Under cloudy moonlight, the Mississippi delta was a haze of black and gray—a photographic negative of tall oak trees and flat fields, the silhouettes of riverside homes on the horizon. Crickets chirped. An owl hooted. I rolled over in my sleeping bag and shut my eyes. I rolled over again.

I'd left New Orleans a few weeks prior and was struggling to continue.

For a while, the city seemed so hopeful—the helpfulness, the community, the unified goals, the unadulterated ambition. But it proved not so. Conditions were worsening, violence was on the rise... I had to leave.

After a stint in a Metairie garage where a fellow Ninth Warder hooked me up with a job doing oil changes, I migrated to St. Tammany Parish. There, I bought a few used chainsaws with another of my New Orleans friends. We made a bit of cash clearing trees for white suburbanites.

Combining funds with a platoon of other desperate men, we discussed plans to leave for the Midwest, where we hoped to find agricultural work. But, with bags packed and gas tanks filled, one by one the men dropped out, unwilling to stray too far from the safety of family and familiar geography. Friendless and under-funded, I headed north in search of labor.

I was awake and anxious in the middle of a hot spring night, and toads croaked in the weeds around me. It seemed like ages ago I'd set out. I'd wanted to learn what I could about America, but instead I was winding up embittered toward it. I unzipped my sleeping bag, stayed on my back for a few minutes thinking, then rose to my feet. I couldn't fall asleep. I walked down the dirt road toward the shoreline.

I was going to swim in the Mississippi—America's River Jordan. I was going to do what had been denied me before. I'd break away from the land so I could see the shores—America on either side. I'd submerge myself in the cool water on this hot night. A chill ran up my spine.

A row of dense trees blocked the water's edge. I crossed through the side of a farmhouse lawn and bounded down a steep hill. A simple, white wooden fence divided a grassy lawn from the riverbank. I came to a halt at the edge of the property and looked over the white two-by-fours into the darkness. Faintly, I could hear a dog barking behind the glass of the home's distant rear window.

I had one foot over the fence when the floodlights came on. The backdoor burst open. A wolf-like hound bolted toward me. I froze. In no time flat, the dog was standing just a hair away from me, growling, lips curled back to show long triangular teeth. It waited for me to move.

In the distance, the silhouette of a man filled the doorway.

The dog growled, its threatening teeth creeping toward my upper thigh.

The man in the doorway shouted something I didn't understand then turned over his shoulder looking back into the house, shouting louder, "You heard me. Call the police."

A green uniformed deputy escorted me toward my cell at the Cohoma County jail, the gun in his holster slapping his hip with every stride.

I don't remember much of what happened when the police first arrived on the scene and took me into custody. I don't clearly recall the booking proceedings or the paperwork either. Instead, what comes to mind is the soldier walking down a non-descript corridor escorted by an armed guard in drab fatigues.

The soldier had done something wrong. The guards led him to a room and set him before a panel of high-ranking officers seated at a long table.

He stood at attention and answered their questions as they scribbled down notes.

They looked at his records. He hadn't had the greatest reports coming out of basic training. His leave had been taken away twice during his first deployment. Back in the states, after repeated run-ins with his CO, he'd gone through his third Article Fifteen, barely avoiding a court-martial.

The colonel sat squarely in his chair at the head of

the table. "You like to do your own thing, do ya son?"

The soldier hesitated. "Yes, sir," he grumbled.

"A re-assignment might be good for you." The colonel took a long pause. "You're lucky we have a troop shortage."

The officers smiled as they scribbled their signatures across a stack of papers that would send him to the desert where the war was most violent.

The soldier was dismissed.

Still in my own clothes, I entered the holding cell. The guard slammed the metal bars behind me and reached through to remove my handcuffs. I listened to the echo of his footsteps dissipating as he retreated down the hall.

On a stool in the corner of the cell, a man in a threadbare suit faced the barred window. I plopped down on the bottom bunk's firm mattress.

A scrunched pillow lay wedged between the mattress and the wall. A well-worn fedora sat atop a folded wool blanket. I examined the hat's tattered edges.

The man on the stool turned around. "Ya mind not touching that?"

I looked at him and dropped the hat to my side.

"They throw the book at ya?" he asked. He stood up and took the hat from beside me.

I told him it was a mix up.

"Mix-ups, screw-ups, and cover-ups," he laughed. He shook his head and dusted off the hat with his hands. "Have a record?"

I told him that I'd been wrongly arrested in this county once before. I told him about the wanted poster

I'd seen. That they'd let me go.

"Oh. You're a repeater," he muttered with a laugh. He placed the fedora atop his matted gray hair. Then he said to me seriously, "You're gonna be here awhile."

I took a deep breath.

"I've been here before," he offered. "Been just about *everywhere* before." He turned away and looked out the window. "I'm the exception, though. They always let me off."

I laid back on the mattress.

"Food here sucks..." He went on. "You know where they have decent food?"

He didn't wait for me to answer.

"Abilene."

A long silence passed before curiosity finally got the best of me. "What were you doing in Abilene?"

"In my business, you get around," he paused. "Small towns, they get pretty excited when a carnival comes to town."

My brow narrowed with curiosity.

"They get a little upset with us sometimes too... Riggings, scams, games... People beg the sheriff, *do something about it*," he mimicked a high-pitched whine.

The carny's shifty eyes wandered to the cell door and back. He held his hand out and motioned me closer with his fingers, as if about to whisper a secret.

"You know who the only real criminal is?"

I shook my head.

"The guy who doesn't understand the system. The guy who believes it's good versus evil, the guy who runs around pointing the finger at right and wrong... that guy's the problem."

He paused and looked around the cell.

"The sheriff—he wants to keep the voters happy. Good for him. It makes sense. Locks me up for a night. Looks like he's doing something."

He waited for me to understand.

"Hell, I make him look good," the carny laughed. "Every now and then I bring the show to town, cause a big stir. Somebody's gotta give these people wonder and inspiration they'd otherwise have only in dreams. And when people get upset for any reason, then he arrests me... his approval ratings go up, voters cheer. He lets me go. Next morning, next town. I get a week's worth of profit just the same. Everybody wins."

Footsteps pattered down the hall toward our cell. A deputy leaned against the bars, discretely pulling a Coca-Cola from his uniform jacket and sliding it through.

"Pssst. Sam."

The carny stood and grabbed the soda. "Thanks, Deputy."

He tipped his cap as the officer walked away and turned back to me. Then he asked me for the second time, "So... How did you end up in here again?"

I told him my story from the beginning.

Sam could clear up everything. All I had to do was agree to work for him until the end of the carnival season. *That's what he promised.* He would get my motorcycle out of impound and would bring it with us on one of his trucks. *That's what he said.* I could leave with him the next morning. *He guaranteed it.*

"You remind me of my sister's kid," he said, shaking my hand. "And I'd never hurt a family

90

member."

    We had a deal. Hours later we walked out of the cell together.

    When I think about it—because sometimes I do—I can still feel Sam's bear-like grip around my palm, his single-pump handshake sending a tingle up my arm and a jolt through my spine. That was when things began to change.

    If I'd already given myself an elementary education in exaggeration and mistruth, it was Sam who offered me a graduate degree. Sam taught me the art of fabrication—when to embellish, when to omit, how to replace missing facts with distraction, when to pepper a tale with emotion and meaning. Sam put me in front of an audience, taught me how to respond to them, how to measure their reactions, when to pull back and when to turn it up a notch. Sam made me an entertainer. He slid me into the spotlight. I was eager. I wanted to learn.

    Imagine the two of us walking along the midway on a Friday afternoon, Sam explaining my job to me as we watched the staffers set up snack stands and carousels and the Ferris wheel:

    "Now listen up kid. You're gonna have to know how to handle these customers. All these little booths and games aren't enough to keep them coming. Hell, those things are hardly enough to get them here in the first place. These people come to be entertained and that's your job when you run a booth—palm readings or the bottle toss or anything else. Our real job here is to engage these people. Talk to them and keep them entertained, enchanted even."

Sam went on about creating stories, how to make small moments into monumental events. He picked apart what I'd told him of my life, and taught me how to re-tell it.

"Don't say that you *stayed* in the homeless shelter, tell them you *lived* there," he said. "Make's it more of a dramatic turnaround when you become a success. It's not a lie. It's a word choice. Brings out different emotions."

Sam taught me how to tell other people's tales in the first person and, conversely, how to transpose events of my own life into the story-lines of third person characters.

"Just look at all these people," Sam said, waving his hand at the crowds. "Each one of them has a story. Look into their faces, into the wrinkles of their skin, the details. Those stories are yours to tell."

"This part is important," he said. "As long as the customer leaves happy, you've made an honest sale." That was his motto.

I'd never met a man who could sell as well as Sam. He was fluent in all the styles and structures, sound in every technique. Sam wove little sales pitches into his words so subtly, with a tone so confident, so conversational, it was as if Sam himself didn't realize he was doing it. Whether it was one person, or a thousand people, Sam's words somehow seemed to raise not just his own self-esteem, but the self-esteem of everyone in earshot. While in a very literal sense, Sam labored through a life of dusty circus tents, lonely bus rides and seedy motels, Sam somehow lived above it all, often speaking of himself as some type of brave ship captain or modern-day cowboy.

In many ways, Sam was indeed every bit as heroic as he was in his mind. He constantly pulled people out of desperate situations—work camps and immigrant labor lines. Sam picked up a new recruit every time a sheriff held him overnight. Sam accepted anybody, put a tool in every hand.

When they couldn't cut it, Sam left them behind. A clown got too drunk, a concessionaire came up short on his cashbox, a laborer broke his hand setting up the tent... Sam left some of them on the side of the road in the middle of nowhere. He discarded them like used parts.

What he wanted, he said, was an ambitious young go-getter like me.

The sledgehammer hung heavy over my throbbing shoulder. At my feet, dozens of three-foot spikes pinned the canvas tent straps to the earth.

Work had only just begun.

Holding an enormous cardboard box against my chest, I jogged a hundred-yard dash through the rain, and then I turned back and did it again. My muddy boots sloshed through wet grass from the truck to the tent.

I placed the boxes atop makeshift plywood tables. Sam stood atop one of them. From this perch, he sipped coffee from a paper cup and told the other workers where to place the floor markings.

"Two feet to your left. Your left! The *other* left, jackass."

The men scurried into place.

I pulled another box from the cargo truck—tickets, programs and t-shirts inside—and ran it under the high-arching striped tent. I ran back for a box of stuffed animals, a box of plastic toy prizes, a box of popcorn mix, fake butter, soda syrup, and carbonation tanks.

There was more unloading to do. It wasn't even breakfast.

By noon the sun was out, and I was shoveling warm dung from the donkey cages. The scent loomed in the humidity. By dusk, I was running extension cords to light the huts of dart games and milk-bottle pyramids. I bent the sights of new air-rifles with pliers. I tightened the bolts and greased the axles of the Ferris wheel.

Caramel corn, cotton candy, roasted peanuts, funnel cakes—the smell of each wafted by on the breeze, excitement heavy in the air. People entered through the gates. Customers flooded the ticket booths.

Behind a waist-high wooden stall, I inconspicuously heeled the brake on a wheel of fortune game. I took people's money each spin and distracted them with one tale or another while I ensured an unlucky turn with my right foot.

To keep business flowing, I'd close my stand for a minute and walk to the game of a co-worker. He'd let me win, and lines would amass behind me while I easily knocked over three milk jugs in a single pitch. At another booth, I nailed a dozen bull's-eyes with a pellet gun and throngs gathered behind me waiting to fire their shots.

Re-opening my stand, I lured the crowds back by promising double prizes for winning spins that never came.

After losing thirty dollars, a six-foot-four ranch hand from Topeka grabbed me by the shirt.

"Thing's rigged!"

He pushed me to the dirt, and I pulled him down with me. His large frame landed on my legs, and I spun on top of him, catching his elbow in my face, the sharp bone glancing above my cheek. Two friends of his joined in, and piled on top of me until the other carnies converged.

The sheriff showed up later to make his report, and Sam was hauled off to jail. The next day we shipped out for Wichita, me with a purple bruise over my eye and a new story to tell.

Sam caught up with us that afternoon, another new employee with him.

Staring out the windows of our bus, I watched all the towns we passed, all the cars and people. In each new town, I dreamed of the lives going on around me, the adventures I could be having. I could have been the town dentist fixing a neighbor's filling, the local plumber with an illegitimate son, the banker hitting on his tellers.

I watched small-town teenage gangbangers and aspiring rock stars. I looked at their square shoulders as if they were my own, their sunburnt cheeks as if they were on my face, their weary eyes as if I was looking through them. I saw myself in them. Their lives became my own.

Sam lectured me on everything he knew: running a

business, organizing a tour, creating spectacle. I learned everything I could about stage performance. How to script a show, how to open, how to close, how to improvise in between. I even learned to juggle — one of the clowns taught me. Another guy taught me some simple magic tricks. On our off days Sam set me up with gigs in nearby towns, letting me keep a few dollars from each show's take. I would travel alone on my motorcycle, arriving just in time to do my act, leaving in time to catch up with the carnival in the next city. I was a star on the rise.

Sam had high hopes for me and promoted my act accordingly. I saw my chance at fame and money and I refused to let opportunity pass, even when it meant accepting Sam's over-the-top marketing strategies. Once, when overhearing Sam describe me as a "real-life American hero" I shot him a death stare hoping he'd choose another moniker. Sam just looked at me like I was the stupidest person he'd ever met. "Anyone can be a hero," he scoffed.

I didn't feel comfortable being promoted like that. I was no hero. I was just desperate, and foolish probably too. I didn't know why Sam had to be so stubborn. He walked across the room without looking at me, then, just as he was passing through the door, he said stiffly, "all ya gotta do is act like it!"

I was determined to try. I wrote and re-wrote my scripts. I drove for countless hours and through many dangerous situations to play as many shows as possible. I rode two hundred miles through a hailstorm to get to my gig in Lubbock. The next morning, I rode another ten hours through pouring desert rain to meet Sam and the crew in Silver City, New Mexico.

My show drew new audiences to the carnival, so Sam set-up a main stage for my act—a well-lit platform for me at the end of the midway. Sam traded his usual worn suit and fedora for a pair of broad-striped red and white pants and a navy blue long-tail coat. A matching top hat festooned with shiny white stars completed the outfit. In this new get-up, Sam walked up and down the midway carrying lit sparklers and announced that a great performer was about to take the stage:

"Ladies and gentleman ... appearing before you tonight on the main stage is a national treasure ... a performer of worldwide acclaim ... the man who tells the true tales of his adventures through our own land..."

We toured the southwest. In California, a booking agent proposed to take me on. After the season's final carnival in Rancho Cucamonga, I was set to tour the West Coast as a solo act.

Sam was true to his word. When the season ended, he shook my hand and wished me farewell, a proud grin on his face.

Chapter Ten

Autumn turned quickly into winter. Then Christmas came and left. Spring passed, as did the Fourth of July. I didn't notice the change in seasons. I toured California with my act, small theaters mainly, night clubs when I had to.

Sam had taught me well. I changed my name, fully adopting my stage persona. I added a musician to my act, who provided a live score for each scene. I developed dramatic timing and promotional flare. Also, I expanded my performance repertoire to include new first-person tales about some of the people I'd met or seen. I had single-scene stories about a small-town southern gambler, about an innkeeper from India, about a big-city panhandler.

Everyone I saw became someone I could embody in anecdotes or episodic sagas whose story lines I augmented with events in my own life. The runaway who hopped a train and the soldier who faced his first deployment—I invented entire biographies for these two, wrapped up in chase scenes and love triangles. Among the many recurring characters I brought to life on stage, it was this pair my audiences liked best. And it was in this pair that I most saw myself. I portrayed them nightly. I told of their journeys, their heartbreaks, their joys and depressions. I learned to measure audience reactions, and I tweaked my act with each performance, adding more drama, more danger, and more suspense.

Stories began to fill my mind. I could think of little else. I was overwhelmed with ideas and recollections. Alcohol became my lone comfort. I began struggling with anxiety.

I complained if the lighting was too bright or if the stage monitors were too low.

"These lights are killing me. And I can't hear myself up here. How do you expect me to do this?"

The bed at my apartment in Irvine was so soft that I couldn't imagine how I'd ever slept on the ground. I couldn't remember how I used to look, or talk, or hear, or smell, or see.

All I knew was that the name on the marquee was mine. I was the talent. I was going to be huge. I was getting bigger with each new day.

I hadn't ridden the motorcycle in months, and I'd put off taking the bike to a mechanic. For most gigs, I travelled in a van, splitting driving duties with my musician. I screamed at my agent when he scheduled the motorcycle appearance.

The chilly Northern California evening stung my cheeks as I zoomed up Interstate 5. Cars sped past on either side—blurs of headlights and turn signals. A speeding blue Volvo came inches from hitting me. I cursed at my agent.

The engine's roar provided a background of white

noise. I silently rehearsed my script for the night. I could see and hear myself acting-out the story lines I was to perform about a soldier from Arkansas who turned around his career after a pair of field promotions. Now he led thirty men. He ushered them aboard an Armored Personnel Vehicle, strapped himself in, and gave commands to the driver then stared out the window. Dust flicked up from the roadway, the engine chugged hypnotically.

It was like I was watching this golden reflection of the sunset on a desert highway ... only I was seeing it all from the big open door of a moving train. I looked down at the worn jeans on my young legs, the tattered shirt on my adolescent arms, the walls of the boxcar around me.

The horn of a Mack truck startled me. I felt a collision of explosive force. I saw sparks from the motorcycle as it skidded across the road.

I saw the bomb's blast rise up like an inferno inside the APV. I was thrown from the train as it derailed. The motorcycle tumbled against the highway at sixty miles an hour.

Seconds felt like hours. There were noises: blasts, slams, sirens, and silences—the sound of the wind. There was pain, a sharp pinching in my spine, the burn of scrapes and cuts to my arms and torso, and warm, wet blood soaking through my jeans.

Chapter Eleven

The spotlight over center stage is a hot one. I'm still seeing the explosion, the collision, the bent steel, the sparks, the cloud of smoke.

The boy's been thrown clear. He waves the smoke from his face. He stands and looks around him, trying to understand the wreckage. His face is covered in soot. His skin and clothing are scraped and bloodied.

The derailed freighter lies beside the tracks. The pile of twisted steel is almost hidden in the thick gray air, but the boy rushes into the haze to see if others are trapped inside.

The APV is on its side, flames engulfing the engine and cab. Unsheathing his K-bar with a bloody hand, the soldier cuts himself free from the harness. His spine and neck numb with shock, he climbs to his feet.

His compatriots had been thrown against the windows that now face the ground. They lie half buried in broken glass, sand, and loose canteens thrown atop them. The world is upside down.

Glass falls from the window facing the sky as he clears it with the butt of his rifle. Sweat and blood drip from his brow while he lifts a limp body out of the burning vehicle. The soldier drags the dying man by the shoulders across the sandy road. He drags out a second then a third then a fourth.

The soldier limps back for a fifth man but falls to the ground before he reaches the APV. Smoke billows overhead. The thumping rotors of a medevac helicopter grow louder.

There's Sam, looking between the bars of his cell window, watching dark clouds rise over the desert, thick black air dispersing into the sky.

He walks shoeless back to his cot, the tattered cuffs of his red-and-white striped pants dragging on the un-mopped floor. He wads his blue long-tail jacket into a pillow. He stretches out on the mattress. Rolling to his back, he kicks his star-spangled top hat, and it falls to the ground.

I take a deep breath, sensing the audience's impatience. I strain my memory again.

Still in a daze, I heard two pairs of black boots approaching. I felt someone sliding me onto a backboard. They spoke, and it sounded like English.

"Find his I.D.?"

"Can't find a wallet."

"No identification."

They lifted me into a vehicle. Doors slammed shut and the vehicle lurched forward. The paramedics took my vitals and called ahead to the emergency room. The cops ignored my pleas as they drove me to the juvenile detention center. The enemy carried me away to a POW camp.

I opened my mouth, squirming, howling in pain, trying to break free.

A man slapped his hand over my lips.

"Strap him down."

A second man wrestled with the belts that restrained me while he jabbed a needle into my arm.

The theater's silent. My memories disappear as if sucked into a black hole. The screen of my mind goes blank. My guitarist begins strumming a folk riff to help me stall. I remember. I'm in a hospital bed. I'm waking up but can't move my legs. I'm looking around the room. I speak into the microphone.

For three weeks I laid unconscious at St. Luke's Medical Center in downtown San Francisco, an intravenous feeding tube in my wrist. An ambulance had transferred me there after I underwent an emergency surgery at St. Francis Memorial Hospital.

My manager made the obligatory visit and left the obligatory card.

A vase of flowers wilted at my bedside. Half a dozen "Get Well" balloons, their strings tied to the bedrail, sagged overhead. Nurses made hourly checkups. Doctors took notes on clipboards. Save for the beep of a heart monitor, my room remained silent.

The motorcycle had been garaged downtown and needed some minor repairs. My manager, my agent— they had taken care of such matters. They had seen to it that the remaining paychecks went directly to my bank account. Under their names, they had rented me a fashionable apartment in which I could recover before finding a permanent handicap-accessible home. They cancelled the shows, turned down media requests, and, of course, wrote themselves large paychecks before leaving to hitch onto a new star.

But at first waking in the hospital, I didn't have the power to sit up, and I certainly couldn't remember where I'd come from or why I'd taken off on such a journey. A little wobbly at first, I moved both arms. Contrary to the doctors' expectations, I'd later be able to move my legs. I'd regain the full use of my body, chronic pain and some tears in the vertebrae of my lower back the only lasting affects. Soon, I'd regain my strength.

The girls at the bars, the doormen at the apartment, the cab drivers who took me around—no one knew a thing about me. For all they knew, I was an alcoholic stockbroker. I could've been a bond writer hooked on pills. I could've been the son of a wealthy attorney, drinking away his father's hard earned dollar. Bartenders took me for a trust-fund baby living in my family's Nob Hill penthouse. Men thought I was a young investor. And women saw an accomplished artist who'd said goodbye to the workaday world.

I never revealed the source of my money. For a short time, I had enough that I didn't have to look for work. Then after my last big paycheck came, I just lived on credit. When bills arrived, I threw them away. The phone rang incessantly.

"What!" I shouted.

It was my former agent. "I've been talking to some people," he said. "We could have a tour in front of us. That near death experience—we can capitalize on that."

"Stop calling."

"We can make you a hero."

"Just stop. "

"Hey," he said more slowly now. "I apologized.

What else do you—"

"Stop."

"You're making a big—"

"A big *mistake*? I'm making a big mistake? *Am* I? You're the one who left *me*."

"I needed to do my job. I got you the apartment... I... I *apologized*"

"Apologized? You left me for dead."

"Listen to me." He demanded. "*Listen* to me. *You* have a career. *I* can take you back up the ladder. I apologized. Water under the bridge. We'll move—"

"No."

"I—"

"You left me."

"Oh, you're *drunk*!" He cursed me. "And you want *ethics*... You? *Ethics*? What do you care about?"

"Don't you lecture me," I said.

"You don't even believe the stories you tell."

"I— "

"You don't. And you whine because you have to make appearances on the motorcycle. You *complain* because you have to act like the person—"

"Stop."

"—like the person you *claim* to be in your stories."

"Stop it!"

"You're not the person you say you—"

"No."

"You don't even know who—"

"*Stop it!*"

"—who you are."

"Stop it!" I began crying.

"You want ethics? You're the one with no ethics.

You ch—"

"Stop."

"You *used* to be somebody else."

"I'm... I'm... "

"You think you're some kind of *artist*. Huh? A *storyteller*. A myth-maker." He was laughing. "A legend in your own mind—"

I slammed down the phone and fell to the floor, my face hot with tears.

Splintered wooden chairs lay broken on the rug. The kitchen table sat on its side, three legs missing. Chipped bits of drywall were scattered over the floor, the walls above riddled with fist-size holes.

The bruises and scars from the motorcycle crash still painted my skin. My ribs were still tender. It hurt to cry. And it certainly hurt thrashing about at anything I could destroy.

I sucked down the last of a bottle of whiskey. Then I hit the harder stuff.

Eventually, I left the apartment and walked ten blocks to the city's drug-infested, low-rent Tenderloin district. I took a first floor room in a weekly-rent apartment. Then I withdrew what remained in my bank account and gave it to an uninsured cancer patient I'd met at the hospital.

Christmas came. Christmas went. Another Fourth of July approached. Except for the people I occasionally conned for money, and the person who kept leaving past due notices at my door, I don't think anyone even knew I was alive.

Chapter Twelve

My face lay against cold wet pavement. My head
pounded.

Someone shook me. The fingers tightened between
my shoulder and neck.

"Get up. Come on. Get up!" He had a loud and
gruff tone, a few decades of Marlboro tar stuck in his
throat.

"Am I gonna have to call nine-one-one?"

I coughed and rolled to my side. The daylight was
blinding. A few cars drove by on the downtown street.
Large buildings built on the sides of hills shot up
around the four-lane road like cliffs around a canyon
stream.

"Thought you mighta been dead."

I coughed. My throat wheezed. The man wore a
patched sport coat over a white undershirt, all
overshadowed by a beard that fell to his chest.

He hobbled on what seemed to be prosthetic legs,
though I couldn't be sure—his jeans fell all the way to
his shoes. He straightened himself then limped to his
wheelchair where he sat down with a plop.

"Makin' sure you's alive. Might've taken that coat
off ya otherwise," he laughed.

I looked at my weathered motorcycle jacket.

"Looks like a nice one," he said.

I crawled to my feet and stumbled back through the Tenderloin until I found my way back to the flophouse.

A stack of opened mail sat atop the chipped-paint veneer of my bedside table; letters from the New Jersey Transit Authority demanded money for unpaid tolls on the Turnpike; a New Orleans collection agency wanted money for a past-due parking ticket; catalogs offered magazine subscriptions. All the addresses had been scratched out several times for re-delivery.

I'd taken this room under my birth name. Since then, mail arrived regularly, all postdated and backlogged over the months and months. The hospital found me too and sent me bills for my surgery and my ambulance rides. I had no medical coverage.

I pulled a bottle from the pocket of my coat. I took a long swig and fell back against the worn pillows of the rickety metal-framed bed.

I was the pill-popper reaching for his bottle with jittery hands. I was the alcoholic standing in front of the liquor store at seven in the morning. I was the salesman running out of the office to chain smoke half a pack of Camels in a single coffee break. I was the drunk at the pub *every* night, slurring my words until my forehead slammed against the bar. I was the homeless man sniffing glue on the corner. I was the sex addict with a prostitute on speed dial. I was among the wretched, my dreams and my resolve rotting and dying, withering away.

A heavy fist banged on the door. There was a

second's pause then three more knocks.

"I know you're in there."

I walked to the door, my legs wobbly.

"And I know you hear me too..."

The thin beam of light stung my eyes as I cracked it open.

The landlord was a large man, fat and bald with a ring of brown hair. He was Romanian or Eastern European judging by his accent. "You got till tomorrow," he said. "In morning you leave." He spat when he talked.

"One more week," I pleaded. "I've been having a hard time. I can get it... I swear. Please. I swear."

"Morning. Seven o'clock," he said.

I closed the door and retreated to bed.

I pulled the chain on the lamp. On the desk were a few empty liquor bottles, my notebook, my camera, and the key to the motorcycle. Wadded on the floor were stacks of unpaid bills, piles of dirty clothes, a few crumpled newspapers, the wrappers from microwavable burritos, a half-eaten cup of ramen noodles, the molding bread bowl of devoured clam chowder...

I sorted through the old food wrappers until I found a half-eaten candy bar. I ate what remained and switched off the lamp, resting my head on my pillow and shutting my eyes, hoping all of my troubles would disappear in my sleep.

By the time the telephone woke me, I was hungover but mostly sober. Streetlights shining through the bars of the room's tiny window told me that the afternoon had passed. I picked up the receiver and slammed it back down, closing my eyes.

A second later the phone rang again. I slammed it down.

It rang once more.

"What!" I held the receiver to my ear.

I recognized the angelic voice of my long-lost love, the curly-headed blonde. Somehow she'd found me.

She said she'd searched my name in a newspaper database at the library of her grad school. She found articles about a sensational carnival performer in small town southwestern dailies and saw an announcement of legal name change in the public notice section of the *Los Angeles Times*. She entered my stage name into the database and found more articles about my performances. She was impressed by my success, she said. She didn't know why my name had suddenly stopped appearing in the news.

"But that's not why I called," she said. "I'm calling to tell you that I'm engaged. I felt like I couldn't do it without telling you first."

I swallowed hard but told her I was happy for her, and I listened to her talk about her fiancé.

She told me about the wedding they were planning. They decided on a date and the time and place. They wanted the ceremony to be private and coordinated the wedding in conjunction with their honeymoon. They'd fly there first, and then do the nuptials before running off to the resort. It seemed funny, she said, to plan a marriage at a place where so many others ran off to wed at the spur of the moment. Still, they had to book the reverend months in advance to reserve the special day. On and on she went as my heart, already weak, broke over and over and over again with her every word.

We spoke about all the things that had transpired in the three years since we'd seen each other. She graduated from college. Her parents bought her a new car. She took a year off, backpacking through Europe. She enrolled at another large southeastern university, entering a graduate program in philosophy.

I told her about all my travels and odd jobs, about New York and New Orleans, about Sam and how he'd helped me begin my career. I told her about my accident, about my struggle to recover, about the depths to which I'd fallen, about the mess my life had become.

She reminded me of the person I'd been when I met her: passionate, brave, adventurous, determined, my eyes full of dreams and my heart full of fire. She reminded me of the person I could be again.

We reminisced about old times together, about nights on the golf course beneath the stars, humid sunny days, the way her heart beat when she touched my skin. She talked about our farewell dinner, about our tearful goodbye, about the final letter she wrote me but never knew whether I'd received.

It was a quarter after four on the west coast. We had talked the whole night through. She could see the sun coming up, she said, and she could hear her roommate's radio alarm clock and the sound of her making breakfast and preparing for classes. She began to cry, telling me that maybe it had been a mistake to call, that maybe talking to me was like cheating on her fiancé, that maybe she still loved me, the type of love she could only feel for her husband.

"Maybe you're marrying the wrong person," I said. She didn't have to say anything. We both knew I was in no situation to marry her. Perhaps I never would be. She wanted a husband.

She sniffled a goodbye. "I have to go. I don't think I should talk to you anymore."

I listened as she hung up the phone, and I sat in silence for what felt like a never-ending moment, the sense of strength she'd renewed in me now entwined with heartbreak.

With the morning's first light filtering between the bars on the window, I gathered my few things and walked out the door. Scattered on the floor remained a few plastic lighters, the discarded liquor bottles, and piles of un-opened mail. I left no forwarding address.

At a nearby diner, I overheard two men discuss a job opening. Following the lead, I hitchhiked to the suburb of Antioch where I fibbed my way into a maintenance position on the dock of a houseboat community in exchange for a stipend and free lodging in a leaky cabin on the starboard side of a dilapidated fifty-two foot Patio Cruiser.

Away from whiskey—and all the other substances I'd been running through my veins—I was able to see things more clearly. The work was good for me, provided structure, and cleaned me up. I found my motivation again. Slipping off during work hours, I built a marketing plan and a tour schedule. I solicited talent agents by phone.

" ...Yes, you remember correctly. That's me... the storyteller."

"We know all about *you*—hard to deal with, whiny, a real prima-donna. We don't want you... Your last agent told me you were a violent alcoholic, that you wrecked an apartment under his name. There isn't a place in California that will put you on stage."

When I failed to find an interested partner, I called small, out-of-state venues myself.

"We're sorry, but we can't just book performers we've never heard of."

Never heard of? I picked my ego off the floor and masterfully handled the objections, using all the sales techniques I'd learned in New York. "If I was you, I might say the same thing but..."

At night, I snuck into the business office and wrote my own press releases. I mimicked Sam's words and style, figuring the publicity generated would be worth it—even if it made me feel like a fraud. I emailed and faxed the releases to newspapers, television stations, and publicity firms.

It wasn't long before the dock owner realized how little I was doing for him.

"I came down this afternoon and noticed that half the pontoons hadn't been plugged!" the managing partner screamed in my face. "They're taking on water— some of the boats are barely afloat. I checked the duty list and saw you haven't even emptied a single septic tank!"

By the next morning, I was on a bus to St Helena. There, I'd take a job working the grounds at a vineyard.

I quit the vineyard job by the end of the month, but not before bankrolling myself for the road. I'd earned enough money to get my motorcycle out of the garage in San Francisco.

With a few dollars in my pocket and a blonde still on my mind, I loaded up the dented motorcycle and headed north.

Chapter Thirteen

The boy stepped quietly through the tall grass, his weathered boots leaving hardly a print in the weeds. He felt only a slight tightness in his right knee. His back barely hurt at all. Gone were the bruises on his rib cage.

The boy spent the last few weeks nursing his injuries, hiding out in swimming pools and museums, sneaking into movie theaters, sleeping in the park on rainless summer nights.

Now, with his body recovered, he walked back toward the railroad tracks. Cutting across an open field, he broke into a dead sprint as a train pulled out of the rail yard. Huffing and puffing, the boy grabbed hold and pulled himself aboard. The world was his again.

He turned around and looked out past the green pastures, seeing in the distance trees that were older than the nation itself. He saw the possibilities of all the people he'd yet to encounter. He saw a road, a squiggly black line cutting across the land.

With a hiccup, the boy held his open palms against his stomach. Maybe it was just motion sickness. Maybe it was just his nerves after such a long hiatus. Or maybe it was just his own psyche, so overwhelmed by the vastness of the land, so overtaken by the power of his ambition that he suddenly made himself ill.

The boy leaned his head out the doorway, wind blowing through his hair as his mouth opened and his stomach emptied.

I drove for days through the bad weather and stopped when the vomiting began. I'd caught a fever leaving California in a storm of cold rain. Now that the storm had passed, I cowered on the sidewalk near an Oregon gas station

A gray haired man cut between two gas pumps, carrying an empty metal thermos into the convenience mart. The old man saw me on the curb as he approached the store.

"Good God," he muttered under his breath, turning away quickly.

My eyes felt like they were bleeding. My throat was raw. My head pounded.

Then came the blood.

I hacked a lung-crunching cough and spat up red mucus on the sidewalk. I rolled to my side and held my stomach. I didn't have the budget for a motel, let alone a doctor.

Inside the convenience store, I guzzled water from the bathroom sink. And splashed some water on my face in front of the mirror. Black leathery circles surrounded my eyes. I shivered and warmed my fingers beneath the blow of the hand dryer.

Outside, I hid myself in my sleeping bag between my motorcycle and a dumpster at the side of the gas station parking lot.

The teeth-chattering cold raised the hairs on my

arms.

The pavement was hot. I was sweating.

Loud tires against the highway sounded like they were just feet away. I curled in a ball, afraid the vehicles would run me over.

The world was spinning. I was nauseous.

That was the worst of it. By the time I hit Portland, I felt almost normal. On a Seattle stage I was heckled and booed. In Spokane I was laughed at.

But by the time I drove into Couer d'Alene, Idaho, local newspapers had picked up on my press releases. A few townspeople recognized my bike and greeted me in the street.

They cheered me as I came on stage. They hugged me as I left. The gig went so well, I began using it as a rubric for future gigs; sending the same press releases, planning around the same time table, giving similar interviews, booking similar venues, and keeping my entire performance simple, almost one dimensional.

With no management, I was responsible for everything—booking venues, writing press releases, coordinating interviews, planning routes, budgeting... I invested countless hours querying publicists, agents, and managers. No one would take me. I continued on my own.

Bad weather often threw off my entire tour schedule. I missed shows, wasted money on shelter, and spent hours twiddling my thumbs beneath the awnings of roadside barns.

When weather or traffic or poor planning held me up, I found myself creating new stories while talking to theater managers, bar owners, and newspaper reporters. The truth was never good enough for me. I didn't want them to know that I was just a one-man operation, fighting for every bit of publicity, barely able to keep my career alive.

If I missed gigs, I blamed it on larger-than-life climate conditions. I paid attention to national weather news. Wherever the last flood or blizzard was, that's exactly where I'd just been stranded. If I missed interviews, I told the reporters that it was my publicist's fault; she'd overbooked me. I had an excuse for everything, each a self-aggrandizing lie meant to cast me in a more powerful light.

Travel, weather, scheduling, finances—nothing was predictable. I had a workable but overall unreliable system for booking gigs and getting press. First I found venues in phone books: coffee houses, theaters, and bars. I called them, telling them that the local paper had agreed to run a feature article on my show, that I just needed a stage to book my act. If they accepted, I called the local paper and sent them a press release announcing my tour, my show, and my arrival into town. When a newspaper picked up on my story, I could expect a full audience and to pocket anywhere between two hundred and five hundred dollars. When I appeared on the local television or radio shows, I was a small town superstar.

When my press releases went unnoticed, however, I was lucky to make enough for dinner if anyone paid me at all. Theater owners would yell at me, bar managers would threaten to have me arrested. Nothing made a venue operator angrier than a near-empty auditorium when I'd assured them a capacity crowd. Some of those nights, after being berated by whichever businessman I'd disappointed, I'd end up sleeping outside.

I was a desperate man, afraid of nothing, open to all opportunities. If someone offered me a few nights lodging or a few days of handyman work, I'd sometimes reschedule my gig in the next town.

I accepted all sorts of offers—a labor stint at a North Country ranch, an escapade with any pretty young girl flashing me a hotel room key, a weeklong stay at the house of an elderly couple. I was the lost romantic to swarms of women, the rambling son to bevies of parents, the center of attention to whatever crowd I stumbled upon.

In Boise, a coed group of National Guardsmen took me out after my show. They paid my tab at the bar and bought me a hotel room downtown. In a game of escalating dares, we ran naked through the hallways at three in the morning, pushing and tripping one another, our young naked bodies falling to the carpet.

Motorcyclists, meeting me at gas stations and often knowing nothing of my identity, invited me to rallies or to accompany them on scenic drives. I always accepted.

"Hey, you there on that motorcycle. Come check out my ride. You look like you've been goin' a ways. You ridden that good mountain road up around these parts? Heck, I'll take ya!"

Or, "Say, Jack Kerouac, ya got anywhere you're stayin' around here?"

Or, "Got any place to eat dinner?"

119

"Hey, you with that American flag helmet! Follow us to the rally if you want."

"Yo, motorcycle man, wave to my children. Stop at McDonald's with us. We'll buy you a burger."

And of course, "Say, Captain America—God, I bet you've been a lot of places. I got a few questions..."

The things people said never ceased to fascinate me. Eating lunch in roadside diners, truckers would sit down at my side. They opened up to me. After all, we were of the same breed: born to ride solo on the highways.

Adamant listeners to AM talk radio, truckers' conversations would always lead to politics. At some point, one suspicious fellow would inevitably whisper about some private theory.

"...Well, that's the big secret behind 9/11. The government doesn't want you to know, see."

Or, "...And that's why those *same* companies are making the military's weapons. I did a tour in the Marines—I remember that stuff! Why do you think AIDS has gotten so big?"

And always, "...You can't get this information from the TV news. The government's got it locked down."

A mustached trucker in a plaid shirt once jotted something down and handed it to me.

"That's my phone number. But when you call, remember it's bugged. Don't say anything you don't want the Feds to hear."

He tore another napkin from the dispenser, looked over both shoulders then scribbled a few lines.

"This is my address. You get to Montana, we got a lot to talk about. I already mentioned Roswell. I got some videos you need to watch."

Strangers were always engaging me, especially when they'd seen me in the newspaper.

Walking across a motel parking lot in Eli, Nevada, a man in a white collared shirt and a green sun visor stopped me to chat. "Let me just ask you the *big* question," he said. He planted his sandaled feet firmly in the desert sand. "Do you accept Jesus Christ as your savior? ...hmm?"

Performing in a coffee shop, I was approached by a local artist: "I've got this novel I wrote. It's mind-blowing. I mean..." This over-caffeinated, darkly dressed man shoved a stack of pages into my hands. "I'm giving this to you to read. I think we can do something together. You can write the forward if you want. Or give it to a publisher for me. Do you know anyone you could put me in touch with?"

Musicians wanted me to hear their songs. Painters wanted me to see their sketches. Poets wanted me to read their haikus. Mothers wanted me to inspire their children. Inventors wanted me to market their ideas.

When I exited a stage, people came to shake my hand or get an autograph, or chat. They had tips for adventures I needed to experience, stories I needed to create, and theories I needed to explore.

In Utah, a gray-haired couple asked me to sign a photo from their local paper. In North Dakota, a forty-year-old man wanted me to look at pictures from his motorcycle trip to Florida. In Wyoming, a twenty-one-year-old brunette wanted to take me out for a nightcap.

In Nevada, a barrel-chested old-timer shook my hand.

"There's some *stuff* you need to check out while you're around these parts."

He pulled a map from his pocket and handed it to me. He pointed to a vast desert, marked by a big blank spot on the map.

"That's the place," he said. "That's where you need to go."

Chapter Fourteen

Golden dunes reflected the late afternoon sun. Heat waves wrapped around boulders and hung over the road. With the exception of a few stony peaks, there was nothing but rolling hills of sand as far as I could see.

I wasn't planning a trip to Death Valley. In fact, it was hundreds of miles out of my way. But my show was canceled in Winnemucca, Nevada, and I had two days to kill before driving to Las Vegas for my next gig. So I figured I might as well go see what that crazy old man from Reno was talking about.

"The ghost of Jesse James," he'd told me. "Jesse and the boys would hide out there from the law. Lay low in a cave somewhere until the rangers were too dehydrated to move, then walk up to 'em point blank, shoot 'em the face. A lot of people say James was killed in Missouri. That's *garbage*. He escaped to the desert to take revenge on his conspirators."

It was all pure hokum, of course, but it wasn't like anyone could prove him wrong. He went on.

"But the most dangerous ghosts in Death Valley," he'd said, waving two fingers in front of my face, "W-W-*Two*." He went on about a group of German POWs. "There were three of 'em. The most cold-blooded killers in the German Army. US government left 'em in that desert to *starve*, their bodies never found... Don't believe me? Explain this: Two dozen unsolved *violent* crimes every year to lone travelers in Death Valley. You can look it up!"

The man's stories didn't scare me. I had no reason to be afraid... at least not at first.

About ninety miles into the valley, my three-gallon gas tank was running low. I had maybe thirty miles of fuel when I finally found a gas station.

My boots met the gray cinder of the parking lot. I looked around. Yellow tape around the pumps, the service station windows covered in sun-beaten plywood—the gas station was abandoned.

I pulled the map from my pocket—no other gas stations listed for a hundred miles.

Nightfall was coming.

I paced on the gravel. I had no water, no food, very little gas, and a show to perform in Las Vegas the very next day.

I looked up to see something in the distance... to the left of the dune, between the red boulders...

A mansion.

I told myself it was a mirage. Then it came to me. I remembered a story about an early-1900s con artist named Death Valley Scotty. Sam had told stories about him at the carnival, "used to run with Buffalo Bill Cody." The old man in Reno had mentioned him too.

Scotty conned investors out of millions by making claims on non-existent gold mines in the desert. According to Sam, the gold claims were real; Scotty was just hiding the treasure. In 1954, an eighty-one year old

Scotty was on his way back into town. History claims he was headed for a doctor. Sam said otherwise: "Scotty was about to die and he knew it. He was on his way to deliver his treasure map to his last and only friend when he was *ambushed*—car jacked at a stop sign and *strangled*, the map ripped from his dying hands. The robber pushed the car into a ditch, and when the cops found Scotty, they saw an elderly man and assumed he died behind the wheel."

I walked to the castle through the desert sands, hoping someone might be living there who had gas to spare, water to drink, or a phone to use—or at least a place to sleep for the night.

I heard footsteps behind me. I turned. Nothing.

I kept walking, the red sunset behind me.

Entering the property through an open iron gate, I knocked on the monstrous wooden front door. No one answered. I pulled at the knob. It was locked. I walked around the stone building, peaking in unlit windows, pulling on latches.

I heard footsteps again. I turned. I opened my mouth to scream.

It was only a coyote, thin like an unfed dog and just ten feet behind me, as if it had been stalking me.

I walked around the side of the mansion, put my hand on the backdoor's knob and gave it a twist. It opened.

"Hello," I called, but to no reply.

I walked in, slowly tiptoeing across antique wood floors, purple twilight filtering through the dusty windows.

The dining room—a huge dust-covered wooden

table in the center, gold goblets and white china—was set for a food-less feast. Nineteenth-century tapestries hung on the walls.

I tiptoed past a knight's armor erect in the corner, past a gold sword hung on the wall. I tiptoed up the creaky stairs.

At the top of the staircase, I creaked open the first door. I peaked my head in slowly.

On the mattress lay a pile of sheets balled with dirty laundry. On the nightstand stood a stack of dirty dishes.

"Hello," I called again. "I'm just a lost traveler looking for help."

No response.

I raced down the stairs, past the tapestries and the dining room table, and into a dark corridor.

Where am I?

I turned around, and met a large figure standing before me. My heart came to a stop. It was only the suit of armor.

I found the exit and sprinted out, leaving the door ajar and the house marked with my sandy footprints.

I ran for a few feet then stopped. There, in the sand below me—fresh tire tracks. I looked for a vehicle. Nothing.

I sprinted to the bike, shoving the key into the ignition.

Then, from the darkness, a pair of headlights hit me like a freeze ray. A truck came driving down the dune.

The four-wheel-drive SUV stopped in front of me. I awaited a monster-like man. A cop. Or worse, a criminal presuming I was spying on him.

The door opened. A lady climbed down, curly white hair on her head. She looked like she was the grandmother from a Norman Rockwell painting.

"How are you tonight?" She introduced herself as a caretaker for the National Parks Service. She explained that Scotty's Castle was used as a museum in the summers. But during the winter, she lived there alone. She had no idea I had been inside.

I told her I was looking for a gas station.

"There's a filling station forty miles that way," she said, pointing further down the two-lane desert highway. She climbed into the vehicle and drove back toward the mansion.

Soon, she'd see the open door. She'd see my sandy footprints. She'd see the kicked-up rug. She'd see her unlatched bedroom door.

I had a two-week beard. I hadn't showered in two days. My motorcycle was piled with everything I owned. I looked like a man on the run from the law; a man looking for refuge in the nation's lowest, hottest, driest, and least-populated place.

She'd assume the worst.

Maybe if I'd taken the time to explain everything... maybe if I'd told her I'd gone inside looking for help. But I hadn't said any of that and she'd driven away and now I was panicking. Now it was too late. I'd already started the bike and I'd sped off down the road.

It was all wrong.

The soldier was propped up in the bed of some makeshift American hospital in the desert reading the witness statements on the After-Action Report from the APV bombing. He couldn't believe his eyes. The document didn't mention any of the details that had been running through his memory.

According to the paperwork, the APV boarded at 1400 hours on a hot September day at an undisclosed desert location. Approximately two hours and twenty minutes into the transport, the vehicle struck a roadside bomb, bursting into flames as it fell to its left side. Only five of the thirty soldiers onboard survived the crash. Of those who made it, three were knocked unconscious in the collision. The fourth was lucid but had been paralyzed in the crash. All of their statements were brief, devoid of detail and recollection. None of them remembered much except the flames. The rest of the report—the time and the location of the explosion—had been filled in by the medevac squad.

The soldier reread the pages. Nowhere were the events he remembered. He stared at the empty half page allotted for his report on the bombing. He picked up a pen that had been resting on his chest and quickly scribbled down his statement.

It was a sunbaked afternoon. Since sun up, he and his platoon patrolled steep sands. They'd been on the front lines for three months, and the APV was their ride back for a week of rest and relaxation. The soldier supervised his men as they boarded the vehicle. He accounted for his squad. Then, he took his seat and popped three codeine-laced sleeping pills—contraband he'd snuck in country in an Aspirin bottle, just in case he needed to medicate away some pain, whether emotional or physical.

The soldier was asleep for nearly two hours when the explosion woke him. He was so groggy when he came to that he felt completely drunk, as if in the haze of a dream. Of all the soldiers aboard the vehicle, he'd been the only one to rise from the crash unscathed, the only one unhurt by the flames. Dazed, he climbed to his feet. He listened as his comrades shrieked in pain. He saw the expressions on their pleading faces, but the soldier couldn't save everyone. He looked for a timeless instant at the names on their breasts and the panic in their eyes. He stepped over Ibanez and Miller and Stevens. He chose to pull out the least injured among them, the ones who stood the best chance of survival. He based this split-second decision on damage assessment, hadn't he? He stepped over Stevens because his legs were blown to smithereens, not because Stevens was a sorry excuse for a patrol leader, not because he had argued with him and accused him of disrespect. And he passed over Ibanez because the man wasn't breathing, not for any other reason. He didn't have time to attempt CPR, right?

The soldier's statement spilled over the allotted half-page and onto an auxiliary sheet. He wrote down everything he remembered, incriminating himself first for taking the contraband narcotics that had limited his capacities, then for choosing who to save based on his own subconscious biases, judging the worth of each man's life.

The soldier reread his statement. His heart racing and his breaths shortening, the soldier crumpled up the pages. He ripped them apart frantically. He could let no one see. By the limited accounts of the four other survivors, the soldier was the hero, the lone able-bodied savior who pulled them from grim death.

In a panic, the soldier looked for a place to hide the papers. In search of a wastebasket, the soldier painfully twisted his bruised torso. He wasn't supposed to leave the bed but he saw a trash can at the other end of the room. Quickly he hobbled toward it, his sheets spilling off the mattress behind him as he reached into the narrow receptacle and hid the torn and wrinkled report beneath discarded tissues and disposed examination gloves. When the clerk came for it, he'd tell him he never received it; the corpsman must've moved it while he was sleeping.

He heard the corpsman coming from down the hall. The soldier panicked now as he limped anxiously toward his bed. His foot accidentally kicking the wastebasket—balled-up tissues scattered across the shiny floor.

"What was that bang?" the corpsman asked from the next room.

The soldier lunged into bed, yanking the sheets up from the floor and tucking them around his body just in time to feign sleep as the corpsman entered and stared at the tipped-over wastebasket with the soldier's private crimes hidden inside.

Certainly I'd be found out. How long did I have before the old woman called the cops? They'd respond immediately. How long before a goon squad of State Troopers, Park Rangers, and law-enforcement brass would start a manhunt across the desert?

What would they do to me? Would I get locked up

like I had in Mississippi—without anyone bothering to get the facts? Would they hold me for hours and not listen to a word I said? If they found me, they'd at least hold me long enough to run my warrants, dig up my unpaid traffic tickets and hassle me about having legally changed my name. I couldn't afford an attorney if I was to need one, and on top of it all I had credit card debt, past due hospital bills, and in the back of my mind... three years of unpaid income taxes. It wasn't that I had any opposition to paying my taxes, it was simply that I'd been too ignorant and too irresponsible to even make the annual filings. If the law got their hands on me, at the very least they'd hold me long enough to miss my dates in Vegas. I couldn't let that happen.

The sky was black. My headlamp provided the only visibility. The engine was all I heard.

Then, about thirty miles down the road, the engine cut out, and I rolled to a stop.

My hands were so slick I could barely hold the bars to push. Sweat dripped from my beard.

Then the battery died, and the headlight went out. I could see nothing, not even the yellow line of the road. A coyote howled. I imagined snakes and scorpions crawling on my corpse in the desert sand.

I remembered the old man's words: Jesse James, the three Germans, two-dozen unsolved violent crimes on lone travelers every year.

The coyote howled again, and I began to push the bike.

Headlights appeared on the horizon then sank into the desert and again the night was black.

Then they reappeared, closer this time. Once more, the night fell dark.

I pushed. I don't know how far. I don't know how long. My back ached.

The headlights reappeared again and kept coming. I slid the motorcycle into a ditch and ducked beside it.

As long as it wasn't a squad car, I thought, this could be my lucky break. I was desperate for help. The car grew louder. The lights got bigger, brighter. It was a sedan... no siren on top.

I leaped into the road. The car screeched to a halt and I ran to the window.

"I need help. I'm out of gas. I've been pushing for hours. I'm alone without water!"

The driver looked frightened—I watched him take in my two-week beard, my awful body odor, my jeans and t-shirt saturated with sweat and road soot.

He mumbled something to his passengers, their speech quick, their tone skeptical.

"I've been on the road for months," I told them.

They looked at one another in the green glow of the dashboard, terror on their shadowed faces.

"I've been through thirty states."

They looked at one another again and mumbled something I didn't understand. The driver's window buzzed as he pressed the button, rolling it up.

Then I recognized something... the three men in the car... their accent.

"Sprechen Sie Deutsch?" I shouted.

They did. And as though believing that no one speaking German could be of any harm, they flung open the rear door.

"Ja!" They laughed as they motioned me into the backseat.

I looked hesitantly at them.

"We're lost," they explained in their broken English.

They helped me get the bike refueled, and I led them out of the desert. I'd make it to Las Vegas on time.

Chapter Fifteen

Public Records from the State of Nevada prove I never did get married there. I know this because I checked. Even with the help of police reports and the stories told by receipts found in my pockets, my forty-five days in Las Vegas remain a blur.

In a report by the Las Vegas Metropolitan Police Department, Reverend Steven Wallace of the Silverbell Wedding Chapel alleges that a man matching my description interrupted his seven o'clock ceremony on February 9th. The filings claim that the man kicked open the chapel door, sprinted to the altar, grabbed the blonde bride by the hand, and took off with her, running out into the streets.

Witnesses standing outside the chapel affirm that the bride left willingly and was chased by the groom across Las Vegas Boulevard, then into the lobby of the Bellagio Hotel and Casino.

Members of the hotel's staff confirmed that a man in a tuxedo chased two people—a male in a motorcycle jacket and a female in a wedding gown—through the bar and across the card room where they disappeared into a crowd. By the time police officers arrived, all parties had left the scene. No charges were filed.

Appointment records from a local real estate agent show that I took an unnamed blonde house hunting on two occasions—first to a condominium just off the Vegas strip, then to the suburb of Spring Valley where we saw a ramshackle two-bedroom ranch-style house with a white picket fence. There's no record of us making an offer on either property. To say the least, I couldn't have afforded anything.

According to the registry at the Palm Desert Motel, I lived in a first floor room with a woman for five and a half weeks.

With the help of those documents, I can vaguely remember what happened over that month and a half.

I came to Las Vegas to perform my stage show at the Paradise Lounge, which I did. But I wouldn't be an honest man if I told you I came just for that.

I knew full well that the love of my life was getting married that weekend. She had told me all of that information so excitedly during that phone call back in San Francisco. She'd told me the date and the time and the name of the chapel.

I didn't know what I was doing. I was in love. I had no plan. I certainly had no malicious intentions. She was in love with me too, and I was willing to give her everything I had...

I remember the two of us rolling beneath the turquoise comforter of that motel room, its wallpaper—a palm tree and seashell print—staring down at me as I rolled off the bed and fell to a knee.

I proposed. Her eyes swelled like grapefruits, tears of excitement rolling down her cheeks as she cried like a baby.

I loved making her that happy. It's one of the most beautiful, most clear memories of my life.

During those few weeks in Nevada, I acted as her husband, living out the quiet life she wanted. I listened to her dreams about starting a family. I went to job interviews. Evidently, I also took her house hunting.

If there was any sort of court document or legal paperwork to back it up, I'd be willing to believe that we eloped somewhere—in one of those little chapels on a love-drunk evening.

I was in love with her, willing to give her everything I had... everything except my dreams.

I remember the sound of her voice when I told her I needed to leave.

"Why did you propose to me then?" She was angry. "Why did you come break-up my wedding? Destroy my life?" I saw those questions in her eyes again: *What was it that I needed to do without her? What was it that was so important to me?*

For those few weeks I had convinced myself I could be the husband she desired while still living the life of my dreams. But I knew better. I could stay with her and live her life, or I could leave and continue my own— returning to the road, back to my quest to explore the nation, back to my stage show, back to my pursuit of fame and fortune and whatever else it was I was looking for.

I'd made a promise to myself at the beginning of this journey. This was my life. I had beasts I needed to battle, a path I had to travel, a gauntlet I had to run, a destiny I had to fulfill.

I never should have proposed.

She was crying. She was screaming. She wouldn't let me touch her. Then she was depressed. She was sad. For a moment she understood. Then she cried again.

I remember looking over my shoulder at her as I pulled out of town on the motorcycle. The differences in our dreams had ripped us apart. Fate, romance, her tears...

I loved her. I love her still.

She'd retreat to her husband-to-be, I was sure of it. He'd take her back. She'd have to promise never to speak to me, never to think of me. She'd worry in silence and with good reason.

Driving out of Nevada, I was glad that both of the motorcycle's mirrors were broken-off. The love of my life had followed me to the parking lot. If I'd had to see her again—even her reflection sobbing at the side of the road—I don't think I could've left.

I sped to make-up ground on my all-but-abandoned tour schedule. That night, I made camp on the flattened spot of a mountaintop just a few yards from Highway 40 in Park City, Utah. Snow came down in flurries. My freezing body shivered as if my soul had just been cut from my skin. I was alone.

Looking down from the mountain perch, I wished I could've been anyone else that night; any father at the wheel of a heated minivan, his wife and children by his side. I could've been any hotshot high-schooler cruising in his parents' sports car, his girlfriend riding shotgun.

I could've been the clerk at the twenty-four hour convenience store a few miles down the road, staying up all night manning the cash register and chatting with coffee-drinking customers. I could've been a vacationer, sleeping peacefully at the brightly lit ski lodge down the pass, sharing a room with friends.

Standing to stretch my aching back, I looked down on that picturesque town just as though I was looking down from the window of a passing airplane in the starry sky, like I was seeing my homeland having been gone from it for a long time—like an ex-pat returning to the town where he grew up, or an athlete coming back from an Olympics abroad, or an ancient tribesman reminiscing over his motherland before returning to the reservation, or a wounded soldier being brought home from a foreign hospital.

The next day I made it to Denver in time for a show I'd booked weeks prior. The day after that I performed in Cheyenne. As I deposited my earnings, a new round of creditors froze my bank account and left me with only the hundred and fifty dollars I had in my pocket.

There was a six-day hiatus before a gig in Montana, and nothing but mountains and wilderness in between. My plan for that week was just to escape the daily pains of my life – to get lost somewhere out on the road.

In a sleepy Wyoming town, the neon sign of the Outlaw Saloon projected a pink haze over Main Street. I walked across the wooden sidewalk at dusk and headed inside.

"Another round on me!" shouted a roughneck to his friends.

With a dirt-stained hand he yanked the frayed rope of the bell. The gong echoed among drunken cheers.

An old rock song blared from the jukebox.

A thick man in muddy jeans and a ripped t-shirt shouted to me over the music. "You from Nebraska?" he said. He had a long drawl and smiled when he talked.

"What?" I shouted back.

"The university trip. Geology class."

I shrugged.

"No?" He yelled. "Well you wanna job working on the rigs?"

"Oil rigs?"

"Hell no. Not in Wyoming. *Natural gas.*" He was drunk and appeared to have had just gotten paid. He turned to the bartender. "Another round for me and my new best friend," he said.

"So what about it?" he asked. "The gas rigs? Couple months work. Twenty-five bucks an hour..."

He asked more questions.

For a few minutes I imagined myself working the rigs under some assumed name, renting a cabin and coming home each day black with grime, my hands rough from the pipes. I almost accepted his offer but I had a career to build and a dream to live, however unpleasant the circumstances.

The next morning I woke up nearly frozen in my sleeping bag and headed into the high altitude wilderness of northwestern Wyoming. The weather was colder and the road poorly paved. The forest was more dense and the land more wild. People became fewer and further between. The day shorter, the night longer.

I drove on.

Chapter Sixteen

The slam of his truck door announced the deputy ranger's arrival. He followed the glow of his headlights to the blazing campfire. His old legs limped carefully over the uneven terrain. He called out to the trespasser.

"Anybody here?"

He turned toward the darkness and called into the forest.

"Yellowstone Park Deputy Ranger—anybody here?"

Then from his right, he turned at the sound of a booted foot over a dry twig. I stood before him invisible in the night, bent beneath the burden of an armload of logs and hidden behind a four-day beard.

"I'm right here," I said. "Camping illegally. I know. Do whatever your job requires."

The firelight caught the fog of our breath. The orange flickers showed the lines of his face, the gray of his hair, the sags of his cheeks.

"I hate to do it," the deputy said. "My boss already saw the smoke from your fire. I have to tell him somethin'."

He reached a gloved hand into his dark canvas coat.

"Here." He handed me a Parks Department receipt envelope. "You have twenty dollars?"

I nodded and stuffed the money inside. He asked me to print my name on his half of the receipt. And I did. For the first time since Las Vegas, I signed my birth name.

"I'm gonna try to enter this slip into the system. See if I can get it by the ranger. The fine is outrageous. I won't give it to you."

With the envelope in his hand, the old man walked back to his car and drove back down the dirt road.

When I saw his headlights approaching again, I knew it was bad news.

The old man rolled down the window just enough to be heard and not enough to let the heat escape and put his face to the glass.

He yelled over the hum of the engine, "Get in the truck. Ranger wants to see ya."

"I'm really sorry," he said once we'd gotten back to the main road. "I used to do what you're doin' all the time. Ain't right to make a man pay to sleep in the cold."

"What's the Ranger gonna do?" I asked as we pulled into the parking lot of an oversize log cabin.

"He *shouldn't* do anything."

Inside the ranger station, a lean man straightened his green long-sleeved shirt, tucking it into his matching trousers like a cadet prepping for a parade. He shut the pine door and turned to face me—the accused seated before his desk.

He paced the floor as if mentally rehearsing a speech then looked his brown eyes into mine and paused for a thoughtful second.

"Trespassing on federal property," he said. "Trespassing. A crime. On federal land. You're a criminal."

He sat down behind his desk and sifted through some folders as if looking for the punishment for such an offense.

"This is a crime against the state. You understand that?"

I looked at him blankly.

He pulled a sheet of paper from the folder. He tapped its crisp edges against the shiny surface of his mahogany desk.

"Illegal camping," he said in a low voice. "Unauthorized fire. Reckless endangerment. Where did you get your firewood?"

From the ground, I thought but I was smart enough to keep it to myself.

"I rounded it up in the forest," I said.

"Destruction of federal property." He responded then looked back at the papers. "I could continue. Any *one* of these things could set you back several hundred dollars in fines, a couple days in jail."

He waited for my response.

I sat motionless.

"You pay a four-hundred dollar fine. Pay the twenty-dollar camping fee. Move to an authorized campsite. Give you till noon to clean the site and then get the hell out of here."

I sat bug-eyed as he placed a sheet of paper in front of me and walked from the room. I filled out the form, scribbling a name and a sixteen-digit credit card number onto the page.

The ranger walked back in holding a folded map.

"You'll need to move to an official campsite. You can't just do anything you want out here." He unfolded the pages and pointed to a circle. "Right here, in red."

He dropped the map into my hands and snatched the completed form. He paid it a passing glance then called his deputy in and handed him the sheet for inspection.

In the darkness of the new campsite, I scoured the forest floor on hands and knees. I scooped pine needles and dead leaves, padding them in the fire pit near my bags, and retreated into the tall pines to find some dead branches.

When I returned, I saw the headlights of the truck again. With a boom, the tailgate fell and with another thud the elderly deputy dropped a load of firewood near my bags.

"Wanted you to stay warm tonight. Supposed to get down to ten degrees," he said, igniting my kindling with his Zippo. "You remind me of someone. Look a lot like somebody I've seen, but I bet ya get told that a lot."

"Never heard it before," I said, truthfully. "Thanks for takin' care of me."

We sat silently in the cold night waving our hands in front of the flames.

"You remind me of my son," he swallowed. "Just shipped out with the Marines."

The fire crackled. He stood to leave.

"Drive straight on through into Montana," the old man said. "First thing in the morning. You hear?"

I looked at him.

"The Ranger won't take lightly to that bogus name

and credit card you left on his papers." He walked to the truck and drove away, leaving on my sleeping bag the Parks Department receipt envelope, my twenty dollars still inside.

I got an early start the next day, intending to put a few hundred miles between me and the old deputy, but got lost in a labyrinth of detours and back roads. A pouring rain began, harder and faster until I could barely see the dirt roads that quickly turned to mud.

Cold, wet and feeling like a criminal, I pulled into a motel. Desperate for a bed, I took a room on the second floor; the twenty dollars I'd gotten back from the park ranger paying half the bill. I walked inside and took off my wet clothes. I sat down naked on the bed. It wasn't fifteen minutes before I heard a knock on the door.

I twisted the nob and peaked out. It was a police officer.

"The clerk told us you've just checked in," he said. "And we're sorry but we're gonna ask you to leave." He paused. "The man in the room directly below you was just murdered. The motel is now a crime scene."

I put my wet clothes back on. I walked back outside where a swarm of squad cars encircled the parking lot. I got a refund from the clerk, fired up the motorcycle and got back on the road. It was still pouring rain.

Near a river in the Montana backcountry, a couple in their mid-thirties enjoyed the view from their RV — the setting sun emerging from the dissipating storm clouds, purple in the frigid twilight. To their surprise, a few hundred feet away, someone was quickly unloading the bags of a motorcycle, digging a crude fire pit with bare hands and rapidly filling it with sticks and dead grass. Perhaps, in the safety of their motorhome, they'd never know how cold the night would become. Maybe they'd never seen someone struggle to gather a night's firewood before the sunlight dissipated to blackness. Maybe they wondered what would drive someone to camp on a sub-freezing night without even a tent.

This was my fifth outdoor night in a row. I'd been shivering, I'd been building fires, and I'd been rationing my bread and peanut-butter supply.

Again my canteens were frozen solid when I woke. I was a fool for traveling through the North Country in mid April. I was ignorant of the climate. It was only by luck that I'd avoided the spring snowfalls that blanket the mountainous southwestern Montana landscape sometimes well into summer.

I looked forward to getting paid for my storytelling show that night; getting to stay in a heated room again. I packed-up, wet a towel with ice melted from the fire, wiped the grime from my face, and set my tires toward Dillon.

Then, lost on the dirt path back to the main road, I ran out of gas for the third time in as many weeks.

It was a dusty trail road, somewhere off Highway 20, loosely paved with gravel and well packed with dirt, cottonwood trees and ponderosa pines lining each side.

Tires grinding up the path drew my attention, and before I knew it I flagged down a raised pick-up truck. A double barrel shotgun was mounted in the back of the cab, and a crisp khaki uniform cloaked in dry-cleaning plastic hung behind the passenger seat.

The driver was a prison guard, doing some hunting on his off day. He was nice enough to offer me a lift to the nearest gas station, a thirty-minute drive.

I plugged him for stories the whole way, and he told me about lockdowns and discovering contraband. He told me about the information trade, a pair of new sneakers for information about drug smuggling.

"Those niggers love them some new sneakers," the guard told me as he rolled down his window and puffed on a Marlboro. "The white guys want something different. Time in front of a television mostly."

He told me about tattoos, marijuana, cocaine, cell phones, guns... "You can get anything in prison," he said. "You'd be amazed what we find in some of these cells."

I asked him how he got into this line of work.

"Had an uncle," he explained. "Heard it was a good living full of excitement. Keeps me outta trouble too."

"Outta trouble?"

"Hell, if I wasn't on one side of the bars, I'd be on the other."

We arrived at the gas station. I hopped down from the cab, filled my one-liter water bottle with gasoline, and climbed back inside the truck. It would be enough to make it back to the station.

The prison guard was nice enough to drive me back to my bike.

"I gotta go back anyway. Haven't even fired a shot yet."

He dropped me off at the bike and continued down the trail on a lookout for wild turkeys.

I filled the tank, hit the ignition and took off, letting the prison guard's stories brew in my head, digesting his words and turning them into my own tales.

I barely saw anyone else until I arrived in Dillon.

A brown-haired boy in a cowboy hat chewed bubblegum and joked with friends. A group of kids playing stickball in the street saw the motorcycle approaching in the spring haze. They pointed and started to shout. Here came the man they'd seen in the newspaper.

A middle-aged woman in jeans and a gray sweater worked her way through the small crowd. She greeted me as I removed my helmet.

"Kathy," she said, shaking my hand. "Owner of the hotel. Montana landmark for over a hundred years."

With one arm, she grabbed my backpacks and hauled them up the front steps, shooing children out of the way.

Up a dusty interior staircase—wooden boards creaking beneath us—she led me to a second-story bedroom.

"Only one other than mine with its own shower," she said. She handed me a key and an express mail envelope.

"You must be a real VIP." She paused. "A man sent me this today. Express. His assistant's been calling all afternoon to make sure I give it to you."

I tore the tape from the top of the envelope, pulling the door closed behind me as I dumped the contents onto the bed. A letter, a press release and a calendar scattered across the green comforter.

Dates were circled in red pen, notes under each with times and phone numbers. The press release billed me as a "real life storyteller," a "survivor and refugee of homeless shelters," a "former migrant worker," "a modern day cowboy," and "an American hero."

The letter was from a talent agent who said he'd heard of me through a carnival owner in Arizona. Besides the letter, there was an itinerary he'd made highlighting my next month. The larger gigs were accompanied by television, newspaper, and radio interviews. He wanted to have a meeting with me, to sit down with me when I came through Chicago.

"This is it," he scribbled in black ink across the bottom of the itinerary. "This could be your break."

As instructed, I picked up the phone and dialed his number.

Chapter Seventeen

With big goals suddenly in my sights, I performed to a standing ovation in Montana. The following morning I was Bismarck bound, fighting through a spring storm to reach a North Dakota television station in time for my interview on the evening news. The next day, I powered through a late night show in Bismarck's small auditorium, then hit the road immediately, rolling through the Badlands and into Black Hills, South Dakota, in time for the local morning TV news. That night, I performed for tourists in the amphitheater at the foot of Mt. Rushmore.

Two days later, I was in Nebraska en route to a photo shoot for the Omaha World Herald. I had a show scheduled in town the following day, then two days after that, a TV appearance and a performance in Iowa City.

I pulled in to a large, brightly lit gas station on the way into Omaha.

Walking toward the convenience mart, a group of giggling college girls ran toward me. I stopped, about to retreat to the motorcycle until I realized they weren't clamoring over me after all. Behind me a charter bus was refueling. Fans surrounded the door, chanting and waving their signs, pleading for autographs. It must've been a band or a sports team of some kind.

I paid for my gas, humbly returned to the motorcycle, and continued toward the newspaper office.

Crowds were thin at my show the next day, probably because of whoever was on that bus I'd seen at the gas station. Still, my small fan base grew stronger. Those who came made posters and screamed my name. After the show, they waited to ask for my autograph and shouted questions as I signed. They wanted to know all about the many lives I'd lived: How many miles had I put on the motorcycle? What was it like in New York City homeless shelters? How do you go about hopping a boxcar? Did I miss the house in New Orleans? How did I escape from the mob? Did I still speak to Sam from the carnival? What was the war like? How many lives had I saved? Tell us more stories about being an auctioneer, an electrician, a lifeguard...

It became more and more difficult to tell where the facts of my life ended and where the fiction of my stories began. Fans embraced the tales I told. They assumed I'd lived every anecdote. They wanted to live them too. Hell, I wanted to have lived them myself.

Feeling like a stranger, I signed another poster and tossed the marker back to whoever'd given it to me. I retreated from the crowd across the parking lot and mounted my motorcycle.

Two men in Harley jackets approached as I was about to press the ignition. They asked if I would do them the honor of appearing at their charity motorcycle rally in upstate Nebraska. I wanted to appease them so I could return to my motel. I didn't mean to say yes, but once I did I felt obligated to make good on the promise.

So the next morning, I headed north to perform at their rally.

I knew I was in trouble the moment I arrived. A beautiful brunette stood among a small crowd. She had long tan legs, high cheekbones, and a sparkling wedding ring on her finger. When I looked at her, her almond eyes ignited.

Her husband wasn't in town for the weekend. He was working... or visiting relatives... or doing a favor for someone halfway around the world. She had come to the motorcycle rally with her in-laws.

Her bronze body glistened as she walked in her mini skirt—tall, lean, the goddess of the Midwest. I shouldn't have been talking to her. I had already made my appearance, and I should've been on the road.

In the long afternoon, the beautiful woman asked me about my travels. When the bikers became too noisy, we walked alone across the street, and she whispered in her soft bird-voice about her own hopes and dreams.

My tales sparked a flame in her, lit the wick of an old candle long extinguished. As she spoke, she came to life in my eyes, glimmered so brightly everyone in eyeshot turned to see.

People walked by us without a word, their angry eyes and expressions doing all the talking.

Suddenly the woman became silent. She ran down the sidewalk to her first-floor motel room. I followed, uncertain of what was going on. She sobbed at the foot of the bed, the teal bedspread wrinkled beneath her knees. I sat down next to her and held her hand. I stared at the tears dripping from her lashes. Her curly hair spiraled down over her face and extended to her narrow mouth. She sniffled, wiping the back of her hand beneath her thin nose.

It was while she pulled her hand from her face that I saw the eyes, the nose, the face of my beloved blonde. It was as if she stared back at me; still in love but married to another man.

As much as I wanted to return to her, as certain as I thought I was to nearing the end of my odyssey, as sure as I was that I would soon be able to settle down with her... I no longer had the chance.

My insides felt as if they were being knifed out. Tears rolled down my face.

Then the door burst open. It was her father in-law. He said nothing. He didn't need to say anything.

I was in the hotel room of a married woman, the two of us holding hands on the bed.

I stood to face the man. He was standing before me, his jaw clenched, his fists balled.

He swung at me.

I ducked.

I ran past him and out the door, sprinting through the crowded parking lot where a group of bikers played cards on folding tables.

I raced around the chairs, accidentally bumping between them, knocking tables and poker chips to the ground.

I made it to my bike. It was already loaded.

I took off.

The runaway had become an experienced train hopper. He knew which cars to look for, when to start running, and where to put his hands when he pulled himself aboard. The boy instructed novice riders how to be safe, just as others had for him. More than once, he yelled to a rookie when to start running, pointed where he should place his hands, and cheered as he made the leap from ground to boxcar. The boy thought about these things as he sat alone on the train.

The boy had helped a lot of people. He prided himself on it. More than a few times he'd grabbed the wrists or hands of men who were struggling to make it into the car, saving them from the moving wheels chugging below.

The boy felt the boxcar lurch forward after being still for a long time. The train he was on had come to a maintenance stop in some nameless Midwestern field, and now it was accelerating again. It was very dark inside the train, which was beginning to gather speed. The boy heard the familiar patter of running feet just outside the door. The boy peered out. It was a man in his twenties, he was running full bore and almost had his hands up to the doorway.

"Come on," the boy shouted. "You can make it. Just a few more steps."

The man kicked his legs into top speed, setting his sweaty palms on the metal doorframe he leapt, pulling himself off the ground.

His moist hands were all that kept him from the spinning steal wheels below.

"I gotcha," yelled the boy as he grabbed the man's arms. The man's face relaxed and the boy's fingers suddenly slipped the man's arms.

In a panic, the man clamped his hands to the doorframe like twin vises.

For a split second he hung on, but his grip gave way.

The man tumbled from the boxcar's open door, and the boy shut his eyes as he heard the screams. The boy pictured the man's ankles caught beneath the wheels, the narrow steel cylinders pulling his legs in and under the train, as blood squirted. The locomotive sped on.

The boy wanted to leap out and try to save the man, but the train was only gaining speed. He stood in shock, the screams echoing through his ears, the man's tragic face etched forever into his memory. There was something familiar about the stubble on the man's cheeks, something reminiscent about the man's eyes.

The boy remembered a story he'd once told to a trainload of hobos about the broken-hearted man who'd taken to the road after choosing his dreams over his sweetheart. The boy's spine tingled cold as he thought about the man and the gruesome tragedy that just took place. The boy sat motionless for what seemed like an endless instant. No one else was around to have seen or heard what had gone on. Maybe he could believe it didn't happen.

Had the soldier taken a different seat on the transport vehicle, had he traded places with another of his troops, he probably wouldn't have survived. Often he'd wished that had been the case.

Instead, he played basketball in the gymnasium of the Walter Reed Army Medical Center in Washington, DC. He'd been taken there after several months of recovery at the Red Cross facility near the site of the roadside bombing. Finally, he recovered enough from his injuries to resume light physical activity, though doctors told him he would probably never recover enough to re-deploy. So now, everyday, he dribbled the basketball. He passed to teammates in wheelchairs. He practiced free throws and tossed high-arching half-court shots. When he wasn't with the other injured soldiers in the gym, he was helping them with physical therapy or spending time with those who had a more difficult recovery: the amputees, the paralyzed, the men and women who'd suffered bullet or shrapnel wounds to vital organs, the ones who still fought for their lives after months of operations. The soldier's attitude improved.

Sometimes, in his private moments, when the curtains were drawn around his hospital bed, he wondered why he hadn't been more seriously injured. Sure, he'd torn discs in his back, he'd suffered months of agony and grueling physical therapy, but why had he been spared when so many of his compatriots had been dealt a rougher hand?

Then again, sometimes he wondered if he'd been victimized. After all, of the thousands and thousands he served with, only a sliver had been injured. He was among the few that had been confronted by disaster. Of all the people who'd snuck in contraband—be it pills or alcohol or anything else—few had anything come of it that weighed on their consciousness. Few suffered lifetime debilitations and guilt. The soldier knew he couldn't continue his career in the military. He knew his back would ache everyday for the rest of his life. He knew he'd be in pain during every car ride, every airline flight, every time he sat too long on the sofa or slept in a slightly wrong position. He knew he would always wonder if he could've saved more lives, if he chose the right people to save.

On good days, the soldier didn't concern himself with these thoughts. He tried to focus on helping those around him, on helping himself, on doing his job as best he could.

That meant daily physical therapy. That meant assisting his friends with their treatments. That meant passing the basketball and shooting hoops with those who'd been crippled.

While the soldier practiced free-throws in the gymnasium of the DC area military hospital, a United States senator walked by en route to a photo-op and glad-handing session. The politician would be thanking the troops and praising their patriotism in front of television cameras and newspaper reporters. For months, the senator had rallied for support from the conservative base. So far, his efforts failed to gain traction. The November election loomed just five months away. The politician was desperate, willing to try anything.

He was walking past the gym doors when he first saw the charismatic soldier from the corner of his eye.

He stopped and listened to the soldier talking to the paraplegics about his own near-death experience. The soldier's voice was deep, resonant. His face was young and bright. His words seemed to drip with hope and patriotism.

The senator accosted the next nurse to walk past him. "Tell me about that man in there?"

The nurse told him about the soldier's injuries—sustained in a roadside bombing—how he heroically pulled four of his wounded men from the vehicle.

By the time the cameras arrived for the press conference, the senator had the Arkansas soldier at his side. The politician used the battle-wounded vet as the centerpiece of the afternoon.

Reporters interviewed the soldier. They took pictures and demanded follow-up interviews. They raved about him to their editors and producers—a charismatic and articulate young patriot. They saw what the senator had seen: a character the nation would embrace, a tale the country was always ready to hear. The reporters needed the soldier just as the politician did. As they saw it, it was their job to showcase such a man.

The soldier knew his life was about to change. He had his reservations but he was excited about it. His anecdotes about his heroics, they were growing to myth-like proportions. He was about to become a celebrity.

I was in Minneapolis when I got my big break.

Since the incident with the married woman in Nebraska, I was more determined than ever to make my career a success. My agent booked me as many gigs as possible. I wrote and rewrote my scripts. I rehearsed tirelessly before each performance. I honed and perfected the dramatic delivery of my tales. I became a true showman.

For years, I'd built up my career one story at a time. When I got to Minneapolis, I finally received the big break I'd long awaited. It was early summer, just a week or two after Memorial Day.

The phone rang in my motel room. I answered and

the excited voice on the other end of the line was my agent.

"We have the perfect opportunity," he said. "Two words—July Fourth."

I listened as he explained.

Through some of his contacts, my agent learned that the star pop musician of the moment—an attractive, young, bikini-clad singer—had been forced to cancel her Independence Day concert on national network television. There was a last minute opening for a prime-time holiday event, and my agent knew all the right people.

He read the press release he'd written in advance of the show. He'd labeled me "a true patriotic hero... the voice of America."

He told me that he'd just arranged what he described as "a series of major interviews."

"I'll get you that Fourth of July spotlight," he promised.

He needed me to meet him immediately at his office on the East Coast. He'd already booked my flight.

Chapter Eighteen

The soldier was picked-up by a limousine at John F.
Kennedy Airport, and escorted downtown.

The limousine came to a stop at a brightly lit
Times Square intersection. The driver opened the rear
door. Dressed in a sharp black suit, a public relations
executive greeted the soldier and escorted him to the
television studios.

In the backseat of stretch black Cadillac, I reflected on
my past life in New York. Driving through the Queens
Midtown Tunnel, I imagined what it would be like
seeing the cement-covered city again, its high, wall-like
buildings, confining the narrow streets. I thought back
on the many moonlit nights that I slept in prairies or
tall-weeded fields alongside cornrows, and how I used to
gaze at the stars and miss the metropolis, where the
high buildings and bright lights hid the moon even on
cloudless nights.

As the limousine's wheels rolled over the bumps
in the tunnel, I felt as if I were inside a New York City
subway car again, riding the elevated rails in Queens
where I would watch workmen walk by with their lunch
pails in one hand and their yellow hardhats in the

other.

The morning show welcomed the soldier to their sofa. Live monitors in the studio showed an affable, overweight weatherman interviewing tourists from the Midwest on the street. The co-anchors murmured and sipped from ceramic mugs.

In front of the stage, the production assistant raised his right hand and began a silent countdown. The studio audience rose in applause. The anchors turned to the soldier with a smile and began.

Later, on the set of a mid-day talk show, our hero shared anecdotes with the show's bald, heavyset host. Teary-eyed and speaking with a southern accent, the host stood and hugged the soldier. The host's mustache rubbed awkwardly against the soldier's cheek. The crowd rose in applause.

"This man right here," the host said, pointing to the soldier, "He *is* the American dream... really, he's an inspiration to us all."

Then the host looked directly at the teleprompter. "We'll be right back after these messages."

Finishing an interview for a late-night audience, the soldier left another crowd on their feet. He was a hero that people could stand behind whether or not they supported the war—the good-looking, young serviceman who had dragged his fellow wounded soldiers from the burning wreckage.

The show's producer slapped the soldier on the back as he left the set. Everyone loved him.

Walking across the New York City sidewalk en

route to his limousine, the soldier came to a stop. On the street corner, a man sitting in a wheelchair begged for change, claiming to have a Purple Heart in his pocket. He had a familiar face—deep-set eyes and a strong chin behind a patchy beard.

Suddenly, the soldier couldn't breathe.

Becoming famous, especially as it happened so abruptly, was undoubtedly the most exciting thing that's happened in my life so far. I don't expect anything to outdo the glorious highs of what suddenly felt like an overnight rise after an eternal struggle. I can only imagine what fame must feel like for stars of bigger platforms. For me, even in the limited dose I experienced, fame felt huge.

Platoons of fans circled me every time I made an appearance. Camera bulbs flashed and popped at all of my publicist's scheduled events. Restaurants refused my money. Legions fell at my beck and call, ready to do me any favor—the greater the better. City after city, I was escorted to luxury suites at the finest hotels.

It hadn't been a month since that phone call in Minneapolis, but already I'd gone from poverty to potential wealth. One moment I'd been relatively unknown and the next moment, I was rising to become one of entertainment's brightest stars.

I'd gone from being in debt to listening to six-figure endorsement offers, comparing book deals, and settling with handshakes after conversations about television and film rights.

"Everyone wants what you can give them," my agent told me. "You're a success. You're a symbol of patriotism. You're better than self-made. You're self-invented. Give these people what they ask for. *Show them the dream!* Let them believe in it."

I enjoyed the benefits of doing so. I no longer lived hand to mouth. My agent fronted me a per diem as part of my touring contract—two hundred dollars a day, paid in crisp hundred-dollar bills, just like professional athletes and big-time rock bands get. Men wanted to be me. Women wanted to sleep with me. Everyone wanted a picture and an autograph.

In the days following my national television interviews, my agent put the motorcycle in storage, saving it to be placed in a Hard Rock Cafe or a Planet Hollywood.

Over the next three weeks, we prepared for the Fourth of July pre-fireworks show, which would take place in Chicago's Grant Park. It would be televised nationwide. I traveled from show to show by tour bus, a five-person entourage along with me—a tour manager, an acting coach, my agent, a roadie, and a guitarist to add a live score to my production. Before performing in each new town, we stopped for appearances and photo-shoots.

As if a testament to how ridiculous everything had become, one photographer had me pose on a throne, a cowboy hat on my head, models on each side of me wearing American flag bikinis, each holding a revolver pointed to the sky. There I sat, someone's living tribute to individualism, freedom, and tenacity; a caricature, like a modern perversion of a Horatio Alger novel, but all too real.

Everything was getting stranger; I was invited to

Hollywood parties. I was courted by armies of people wanting to join me on the road, the groupies of actors, actresses, and musicians offering me their free pharmaceuticals—a pill to pop, a special cigarette to smoke, a substance to inject straight into my bloodstream.

Looking back on it, I've got no one to blame except myself. No one else built my career. The agents, the corporate suits, the hangers on, they did their damage, but it was me who affected audience after audience with my tales, filling their heads with the same nonsense I'd jammed into mine.

The truth was: I knew nothing, especially about myself. Still, the people came in droves. The audience, having heard my stories, still wanted more. They wanted more stories about being a train hopper, more stories of battlefield heroics. They wanted more entertainment, more inspiration. They asked me for autographs, and they asked me for all the answers, as if I was responsible for making the world more fair, or for giving them the motivation to pursue their dreams. They acted as if I was supposed to know things, as if I claimed to be a messiah. Politicians courted me to take sides with them on whatever hot-button issue. The leaders of social causes and charities pleaded for my support.

My agent came to me with offers for appearances, performances, speeches, and books. He encouraged me to just keep going, to perform every night—even after I confessed to him that I felt like a confused televangelist.

I take the blame. It was me who continued.

163

At one stop, a bellhop asked to get his picture taken with me. I posed for the shot then shook his hand. As I watched him disappear into the service elevator, I felt a part of myself vanish.

My memories as a laborer, as a door-to-door salesman, as a dockworker— all these former selves I'd been—they all seemed equally out of reach. My life history, my stories of what happened during my time on this—I jumbled them all together for my performances. They came back to me like daydreams that I couldn't discern from truth. Perceptions became realities.

Over and over again, I had visions in black-and-white, or out of focus. I'd see a moving train across a distant prairie. Or I'd see my face on the neck of a twenty-one-year-old kid, my hair cut high and tight, a suit of camouflage covering my body.

Up on stage I sometimes found myself confused, as if I wandered between plot lines and characters, unsure of who I was and who I was portraying.

Often I thought of the runaway on the boxcar. Sometimes, I'd think I saw him on whatever train I watched from the window of the tour bus. Other times, I knew for sure I saw him on a river raft as we drove across a bridge in St. Louis or St. Paul or Memphis.

I saw his life through the eye of my mind. The boy traveled the rails so long he became a legend. New riders who flopped into his open car already knew all his stories. They'd come up and shake his hand. They'd tell the boy all the tales they'd heard of him: that he'd risked his own life to save the starving, that he'd helped travelers of all kinds get where they wanted to go. The boxcar jumpers believed the ridiculous tales, even the ones that couldn't be true. They believed that the thirteen-year-old had given up everything most people hold dear—security, wealth, the love of a good woman—all in an altruistic quest for liberty and freedom.

He couldn't possibly live up to such billing. Everywhere he went people begged for help and advice. None seemed to notice how limited, how over hyped, how shamelessly self promoted, how full of shit the youngster really was.

Surely he wouldn't be able to put up with this forever. I wondered what he'd do. After all, he didn't want to hurt his admirers. He didn't want to drain the pools of inspiration he'd filled for them. And furthermore, the boy knew no other way to live. The stories were his only tools of survival. Maybe he'd continue the masquerade. Or maybe he needed to find out what he looked like behind the mask.

Every dressing room mirror became my enemy. In Cincinnati, I saw my father's face instead of my own. In Indianapolis, I saw faces of a thousand people—bankers, plumbers, doctors, hobos, soldiers, disaffected youth, lawmen, musicians, school teachers, a prison guard. Maybe it was the stage make-up, but I found myself staring over and over again into the glass.

Still, I took the stage every night like a true showman and approached the microphone like a preacher on Sunday morning. I did my song and dance always with fresh zeal, and filled myself with spirit for each day's revival.

I continued right through the end of June and

into July; an arena in St Louis on the thirtieth... an auditorium in Eau Claire on the first... a concert hall in Milwaukee on the second... and, this morning, on the third of July, we arrived here, at this very opera house in Kalamazoo, Michigan.

Chapter Nineteen

Standing alone on the Michigan stage, I've just told the audience everything I can remember.

And when I think back on it, it's the parts that are least believable that seem the most true in my blurred eyes.

The faces of all the people in the crowd are utterly confused through the haze of the spotlights. They're not sure whether to be mad or sad, whether to take me seriously, or to laugh everything off as if it were all the act of a bad stand-up comic. But they look at me as proof of something, as hope or as evidence of this or that. Some still assume I can give them an honest recollection, still hoping for me to inspire them, still expecting me to be their example, to be their pitchman, their supplier, their dealer, their guru of some poorly-defined flag-waving inspiration.

But I know better. I know all the holes in my story. I don't remember where they are or what I filled them in with, but, for certain, I know the holes are there.

A brown-skinned man with hair past his shoulders, two blonde parents with three sons in Boy Scout uniforms, a teenage kid in jeans. Each face stares at me from the audience, so too do all the faces in my mind—all the faces from the mirror. Memories, images, hallucinations run wildly through my brain. I can't take any more. The show's over.

I sprint from the stage, darting past my musician. I run through the corridor, past the bald tour manager, past my agent.

I have nothing but the clothes on my back, but I have a considerable amount of cash on my person. Rushing out the emergency door, I trip the fire alarm. It's dark outside. I cut across the parking lot, through a row of bushes, down an embankment, then sprint for the main road, toward the highway. Behind me, the fire alarm blasts like a siren, and I can hear the panicked crowd rushing out of the building.

I'm wheezing, I'm running so hard; running away from all those faces in the mirror, all those faces in the story scripts, all those faces in the audience, and suddenly I realize that I'm crying, probably because I can't remember my own life except that I've worked so hard and got so lost, and somewhere inside of me is every person I ever claimed to be.

I hear the on-ramp in the distance ahead of me. Cars and trucks rumble from far away. I can make out the long low wail of a transcontinental freighter.

I feel the train's thunderous movement through my boots. I see some men poking their heads through a boxcar's open door.

The train hoppers all swap stories. Soon they'll squabble over who's telling the truth. One man will call another a liar. That's how it so often starts—one person calling another a liar. Then the fighting will begin, usually very slowly. Sometimes they'll start just by talking. Sometimes they'll shout. Rarely, they'll just go straight to shoving. The arguments will wane. They'll escalate again. The tension will oscillate over the hours and days that the men ride together. Friendships will be forged around those who have brought a bag of food. Alliances will be made with those who brought a canteen of water. Deals will be negotiated with those who have a pint of whiskey. In cold weather, everyone will elbow in on one another, each trying to position himself in the rare spot safe from the strong winds of the large open door. In the summer heat, the hobos will snake toward the fresh air, always competing for space and supplies. Slowly and inevitably, animosity will grow, breeding and swelling until someone finally snaps. Then, as it always has, the violence will start. A swarm of men crammed within a limited piece of real estate will battle for resources. The boy will be caught in the middle, forced to take sides.

I continue running, my lungs burning, my legs turning to volcanic ash. Certainly someone's after me—my agent, my manager, fans—someone will track me down if I don't get out of town and fast.

Approaching the highway, I cut across an intersection and weave between vehicles swerving and slamming their breaks. I cross in front of a drab green bus filled with men in uniform. They stare out the window at me as I sprint past them. I can feel their eyes and hear their murmurs. They're soldiers or recruits of some sort, perhaps part of the National Guard, or they're seamen from the Great Lakes Naval Station. They're preparing themselves for combat, preparing themselves for battle, preparing themselves for whatever it will take to become heroes. I look over my shoulder, giving them a passing glance as I run up the on-ramp and onto the shoulder of the highway.

I hold out my thumb at the first car to drive by. No one's stopping.

Of course, *why would they be?* I look like a nut out here, standing in the glow of headlights with no luggage, my face and arms shiny with sweat and tears.

I hear my life rumbling through my ears, through the car horns and highway noises. Through the growling engines and screeching tires, the clicking transmissions and the steadily roaring speed of countless cars, I hear the voices, the voices of everyone talking—the drivers, the passengers, the people from my past. Their conversations fly by at seventy miles an hour, their words mash together in one raw sentence, "......education.........religion.........rock 'n' roll......liberty......government...protest, freedom, patriotism, sex, taxes, drugs constitution segregation raceriotsindiansglobalization— "

The voices are accompanied by images now, of all the people I've met, all the land I've covered. It's all whizzing by.

There's the bearded man at the gas station in east Texas. There's the kid changing his tire. The woman walking alongside the horse. The teachers in Arkansas, the butcher, the rock band, the home owner pelted with mud on the banks of the Mississippi, the fried-chicken waitress in Florida, the immigrants in Georgia, the old man, the innkeeper, the preacher in North Carolina, mobsters in New York, refugees in New Orleans, a carnie and a cop and a clown in full makeup...

Then I see my blonde beauty—her golden hair, her thin nose, and her almond eyes. She's in a nightgown, lavender sheets pulled to her chest, her husband asleep at her side. Suddenly, she shoots up in bed, her eyes wide. Her husband is undisturbed beside her. She grabs her robe from the nightstand, scurrying to the front windows. She sees nothing but the empty street on a late Saturday night.

She swears she's heard something—the revving of a motorcycle, the metallic thundering of a speeding train, the roaring wheels of a troop transport bus, highway sounds.

She stands in silence for a moment, far from the traffic on the busy interstate where I stand with my thumb in the air.

An eighteen-wheeler flashes its brights at me. The air brakes hiss as the truck pulls over.

I run for it, now certain of my escape, knowing that the morning sunrise will bring a wave of reporters flooding the entire region, each one interviewing innkeepers and diner waitresses, all of the newsmen searching for me, handing out my photograph saying, "Yes, the storyteller, that's who we're looking for," while all of the people—the diner employees, the maids at the motels—they'll shake their heads and say, "Sorry, we haven't seen him around these parts."

I'll be long gone. Wherever this eighteen-wheeled beast is headed, to whatever town where no one knows my name, that's my destination.

Chapter Twenty

I hid out in a low-rent motel on the east side of Indianapolis, beneath a cloud of marijuana smoke, beside an anthill of cocaine.

I'd been pumping chemicals into my bloodstream ever since that trucker dropped me off. I didn't know what the hell was going on. One moment I was planning my suicide, the next I was elbows deep in a writing frenzy, trying to scribble down every memory I ever had.

What I'd been able to deduce is this: just five years earlier, I'd had a life as a student with an apartment and an ROTC scholarship from the Navy. I was a backup catcher on the university baseball team. I had girls I took out, a big shiny blue SUV, a large television with a hundred crystal-clear channels. I left that identity behind to travel America, with the absurd idea I'd discover some pearl of knowledge, evolve into a greater person and maybe even find my destiny.

I'd set out to make something of myself, to live the biggest life I could, to become as successful as possible and to help as many people as I could along the way. It had never been my intent to hurt anyone, or myself either.

All I could understand was that I had set out to

learn my homeland. I'd set out to be a force of good in
the world. I'd set out to make a fortune. I'd set out to see
what I could become, to stretch my arms a little further,
to run a little faster, to feel the lift against the bottoms
of my palms as I gained speed until one day, one fine
morning I would...

What had I done to myself? What had this land
made of me? What had I made of this land? Who had I
become? A liar. A charlatan. Over the three weeks or so
since I'd gone AWOL during my Michigan show, I'd
become a suicidal drug addict.

Things had gotten bad. Perhaps the drugs were
going to kill me. At that moment, I would have wanted
it that way, but that's when fate intervened.

My motel bill, pizza deliveries, liquor runs, drug deals—
I paid for everything with cash. When I left that opera
house in Michigan, I had nearly three grand stashed on
me, thirty hundred-dollar bills; much of it lining my
boots. Fifteen days worth of per diem.

As my cash supply dwindled and my desire for
drugs grew, I became more and more tempted to try my
bank account. After all, no one had even come close to
finding me. It had been nearly twenty days since I'd
seen my name in the news. I convinced myself they
must've given up.

America must have already turned its attention to
whatever gimmick it selected to worship next. Surely
people had forgotten about me, and I could live again in
total anonymity. I hadn't been on the national stage
long. By now, I figured, the heat was off and I could
make a withdrawal without anyone caring.

Maybe I made that withdrawal too soon. Or maybe I just didn't account for all the big-shots my disappearance had pissed off, all the people I'd angered with my dishonesty, all the fines I hadn't paid, all the enemies I'd accrued.

Only four hours after I wired myself three thousand dollars to a nearby Western Union did I realize how wrong I'd been.

I was flipping channels on the television in my motel room, a newly purchased eight ball and an ounce of marijuana next to me on the mattress, a bottle of bourbon on the floor for good measure. I was cutting the coke into lines when I saw something flash across the TV screen. I turned up the volume. There, on the television in front of me, was a live shot of the motel parking lot. News vans, lighting stands, and cameras on tripods populated the blacktop. The newscaster, his voice accompanying the video, explained the situation:

> ...Yes, thank you Janine. Live from the east side of Indianapolis, you've heard right, we've found him. In hiding for over the better half of a month now... the infamous stage performer known for his tall-tales of heroics and patriotism has been linked to this low-budget motel. Allegedly, he made some bank transfers in this area earlier today. As our sources tell us, he very well may be inside and there could be drugs involved...

The newsman was right. I *was* inside, but not for

long.

It was only by luck that I was able to escape. The cable news stations, competing against one another to break the story, had found me before the police did. Not surprisingly, they'd fought one another to set-up their cameras and make the first live broadcast, all without informing law enforcement.

In the media's defense, I should say that there were no warrants out for my arrest at that time. In fact, the many efforts to find me were completely disjointed. While nearly two-dozen states had taken up local investigations, and the FBI had begun to look-into my history, no charges had been filed. Each investigation was still being treated as its own affair. The media, local cops, private investigators hired by my former manager and agent—none of them were sharing information. With the events that unfolded at the motel however, everything changed.

As I made my getaway—squeezing through the bathroom window then weaving through the alleys and the backstreets of eastern Indianapolis—police arrived at the motel. As I picked-up a ride with an unsuspecting motorist, the officers ravaged through the motel room's dresser drawers, finding nothing but a Gideon's bible. While law enforcement bagged and labeled-the cocaine and the marijuana they found in baggies on the bedspread, I crossed state lines into Ohio.

In the coming weeks, I'd learn that my pursuers had organized and multiplied. They'd drummed-up charges for every crime I may have committed, no matter how small, and they were ready to take me down.

The people I'd hurt financially—agents, tour managers, television producers—they filed multiple charges of fraud, embezzlement even. They began a media campaign against me, appearing as guests on cable news programs, slandering me, painting me as a potentially violent and dangerous man. One even called me an ideological extremist; though I don't know what ideology he was referring to.

The State of Indiana was using what they'd found in my motel room to charge me with felony drug possession with intent to distribute. The IRS and a handful of states looked into my records and began pursuing me for related tax crimes. Additionally, a prosecutor from Arkansas filed charges of trespassing and assault on behalf of a man who claimed I'd fired rocks and mud at him while trying to flee his backyard—an event he described as a "thwarted robbery." The National Parks Department was after me for my run-ins at Yellowstone and Death Valley. District attorneys in New Orleans had me connected to an anarchist group and accused me of trying to embezzle social service funds. Prosecutors from New York City and the surrounding tri-state area pursued me for unpaid tickets for all the tolls I'd run.

To top it all off, a government task force had connected all the dots of the above allegations to paint me as a highly skilled con man, a possible narcotics trafficker, a potential terrorist... an enemy to the state.

In many ways, living on the lamb came naturally. I was used to taking on new personas, sliding seamlessly into any situation, hiding, bouncing from place to place without friend or family, making up new names and life histories.

The vilification was new though. It was rough and it had only begun. Cable news and infotainment journalists ran roughshod over me. Listeners of talk radio began calling in to accuse me of all sorts of unsolved crimes.

Police bulletins listed me as "armed and dangerous." Reports came in that maybe I'd knocked over a liquor store outside of Cleveland. Maybe I was responsible for that bank heist in Columbus, or that car jacking in Cincinnati.

None of this was true, and ironically the investigation of such reports only cleared my path across Ohio, through Pennsylvania and into upstate New York.

I knew better than to return to any place I'd been, so I was headed for the six states I'd yet to reach. If I was going to die on the road, I was going to die attempting one of things I'd set out to do when I'd begun—I was going to travel through the entire country, the forty-eight contiguous states anyway. This became my single motivation, the one dream I had left to chase, the one cause I could cuddle at night, the sole thing that made my life livable.

Despite the obvious obstacles I faced as a wanted man, I managed to progress across northern New York and into Connecticut. Another five states had issued warrants for my arrest, the charges running from armed robbery to petty theft. According to the newspapers, authorities had linked me to nearly four-dozen robberies across the country.

"What do we really know of this guy?" I heard one AM radio host say about me. "He bursts onto the American entertainment scene out of some mysterious itinerant past. We've learned that he fabricated the events in his stories. Probably every word he ever said was a lie. For all we know, the guy's a blood-thirsty criminal."

Yet as talk like this escalated, a new set of circumstances emerged that enabled my journey. Entering a country store in rural New York after walking several miles along back roads, I was met with a new greeting.

"Just don't kill me," the lone clerk screamed. He'd recognized my face as I came through his doorway, and threw his arms to the sky. "I'll do anything you want. Just don't hurt me."

Without another word he emptied his cash drawer onto the counter.

"Take it," he said. "I won't even tell them you were here."

He stuffed the money into a bag for me.

I was a desperate man presented with an opportunity. There must have been five hundred dollars in that bag. I grabbed it from him, asked him to step into a storage shed in the back, locked him inside and took off with the much-needed cash.

This became a common occurrence. I also began stopping drivers along empty highways. Knowing my face, they handed over the keys to their cars. I demanded that they ride with me, offering to let them out in the relatively unpopulated backcountry where they would have to walk several miles for help, and they fearfully obliged.

With law enforcement hot on my trail, I had to act more boldly. I had more tracks to cover. I had to move more quickly, more erratically even from one part of a state to the next, making it as difficult as I could for authorities to pinpoint my whereabouts and my next move.

Chapter Twenty-One

I began to travel in disguise. With the money I'd accumulated, I bought a whole duffel bag of eyeglasses, wigs, and make-up.

My first disguise was nothing more than a discount pair of reading spectacles, the grocery-store variety. A few days later, from the women's aisle of a drug store, I added multiple shades of foundations and concealers, allowing me to lighten or darken my complexion. I collected an arsenal of hats and sunglasses to shade my face and eyes. Later I added hairpieces—long and brown, short and blonde. I carried a pair of scissors for altering both my own hair and the wigs. I also carried a bottle of peroxide and a bottle of dye.

I progressed into Rhode Island then up into Massachusetts.

My most inconspicuous disguise, and therefore my best and most used, was a pair of silver-rimmed reading glasses, a brown wig, and a navy blue ball cap with the bill rounded and pulled low over my face. I felt safe in that costume and never seemed to get a second look.

Unfortunately, wearing the glasses as frequently as I did began to affect my vision. The low-level magnification wreaked havoc on my eyes, blurring and distorting anything further than a foot in front of me. When I removed them to sleep at night or to wash up in the restrooms of truck stops or fast food joints, my vision seemed irreparably skewed. In the mirror, my nose seemed twice as long. My ears and jaw and cheekbones looked miniature by comparison. Everything looked different. Sunspots dotted my peripheral. Lights seemed dimmer, shadows elongated.

All of this only added to my own already blinding confusion as to who I was. Just as I had in Indiana, I filled notebooks full of recollections, memories, and imagined pasts, and I was rarely able to differentiate between them.

I wrote by moonlight on long, lonely nights in the woods. I wrote while sitting on the side of the road waiting for rides. I wrote while riding shotgun in the late model Ford that took me into Rhode Island. I wrote while in the backseat of the minivan that took me into Massachusetts. I wrote, I re-read, I tried to fit the pieces together. My mind and my past were completely scrambled. Nothing worked.

I wrote about memories of myself as a child, sitting with my father in a small sailboat just outside the harbors of Marina Del Ray, California. I wrote about memories of my boyhood, watching television with my mother in a farmhouse somewhere in rural southern Maryland. I wrote about memories of my youth— stealing bags of chips from a convenience store with my big sister, the clerk yelling at us in Spanish as we ran out the door. I wrote about memories of childhood homes in Kansas and arguments amongst my peers in a

Louisiana seventh-grade classroom. There's no way all these memories can be mine.

Time and time again, after writing until my hand cramped and my mind stiffened, I closed a notebook in utter frustration. Even after I stopped writing, the memories plagued my subconscious mind.

Regularly, whether sleeping out in a roadside field or dozing off in the passenger seat of a sedan, I woke up in cold sweats, having dreamt that I was wading through the swamps of my mind, haunted by the apparitions of who I could've been, of who I never was.

In the darkness of a county park just north of Boston, I dreamt I was an animal on the verge of extinction. On the concrete slab of an abandoned gas station just south of the Vermont line, I dreamt I was a marionette cut from the tethers of the puppeteer and slinking helplessly without those dreaded yet necessary lifelines. In my darkest imaginings, the one thing that saved me was the recurring image of a man on a motorcycle, his face stoic and his body language confident and unafraid. Sometimes his face reminded me of that of the runaway. Sometimes I thought he looked like the soldier, but with longer hair, and a little more age on his forehead, a little more calm in his eyes. It was only during those rare moments when he appeared in my mind that I was granted a brief reprieve from my nightmares.

Nonetheless, I continued on, bearing my cross, carrying my torch.

In the passenger seat of a rusted-out VW minibus, I rode into Burlington to claim my forty-sixth state, law enforcement nipping at my heels.

A strange thing happened as I progressed through the northeast. At first I read about it only in passing glances at the newspaper. I saw snippets of it in the news coverage on television. Then I heard about it on a radio program as I passed through Brattlesboro in the van of the sixty-something white-haired hippy who'd picked me up in northern Massachusetts.

"What we're witnessing here is one of those cultural phenomena," said a radio host. "It could just be a backlash to all the media's demonizing, but a loud group of supporters have emerged displaying their sympathy for a man who, I believe, should be placed on the FBI Most Wanted list."

I tried to steady my breathing. I tried not to look at the face of the driver. The radio host was talking about me.

The driver turned up the volume, listening more closely.

"What do you think?" he finally asked, turning down the volume with his right hand, keeping his left on the steering wheel.

I shook my head in mock nonchalance.

"I think those people are right," the driver said, firing up a hand-rolled cigarette with the car's push-button lighter. "Have you heard any of the reports from the people who can actually confirm they were robbed by him?" The driver cracked his window. "They all say they were shocked by his politeness. He didn't hurt or threaten any of them. None of them ever claimed he had a weapon. It was like they just freaked out when they saw him and offered up everything they had. Some law professor in Arizona started doing his own investigations, already proved that nine or ten of the accusations are totally bogus."

Silently, I stared through the windshield.

"I'm not saying he's never broken the law," the driver said, "but I think he's just gotten unfairly fingered as some sort of uh," he took a long puff on the cigarette, "a public enemy. Like a threat to mainstream society. That's what all this is about."

I'd become a polarizing national figure, vilified by most but admired by a growing minority. My supporters came from all walks of life: hippies like the guy to my left, disenchanted conservatives in the South, disenfranchised minorities in the big cities, north country survivalists, military vets proud of their nation's history of rugged individuality, rebellious college kids, practically anyone who had ever been set free—by rock n roll, by hip-hop, by jazz—they rooted for me too, even if they knew I stood little chance of survival. In fact, that was part of my appeal. I was the underdog in a fight for life, threatened like an endangered-species but, like Geronimo, always on the warpath. I was Hannibal facing Rome. My defeat was inevitable, but my ability to delay it was heroic.

I mustered up the courage to remove my disguise and reveal my identity to the middle-aged hippy at the wheel. It was a good thing I did. He'd followed all the news coverage. He'd been talking with his old protest buddies from the sixties. Their intel had told them that the feds were onto me. From the notes I'd left behind at the Indianapolis motel, authorities had deduced that I was still trying to reach all forty-eight states. Police set up barricades all across the borders of New Hampshire and Maine, willing to wait-it-out until I came to them. But now we had a plan.

With the money I'd accumulated frequenting late night stop-and-shops, we enlisted his friends along with nearly a dozen of their vehicles—sedans, sports cars, a box truck, a mini-van, even a Mercedes—which we then used to ferry me across state lines, their trunks becoming my hiding spots whenever our outriding vehicles spotted a road block, a speed trap, or a police checkpoint. If they ever had any idea of the type of car I was in, it wasn't for long.

From New Hampshire, we threw them a curveball, hiding out in a sympathizer's barn for six nights before cutting back down into Massachusetts, anticipating a higher level of security on Maine's western border.

Then, on a morning in mid November, my entourage of outlaws snuck me into the southeastern tip of Maine. At sunrise, they said a quick prayer of sorts then took off just as I had asked them to, hoping to save them from my own fate.

With nothing but a knapsack of sandwiches, I continued on foot toward the Atlantic Ocean, hoping the nation's most eastern shore might somehow offer me a glimpse into the reality of my past. In the outskirts of Bar Harbor, I hid in an abandoned rail yard as a Veteran's Day parade marched across Main Street, waiting for the crowds to clear before I continued. I heard the celebratory cannons blast. I heard the whistle of the distant train. I heard a trumpet call.

My pursuers couldn't have been far behind. There was no choice but to continue.

Chapter Twenty-Two

A breeze roars from the shoreline and brushes my hair
back. The moisture brings a familiar tingle to my
cheeks. It's the most lucid and complete recollection I've
had in ages. For an instant, it feels like maybe I can
finally make some sense out of it all. The wailing sirens
of distant police cars tell me I don't have much time.

How did all this unfold? How is it that I stand here
now—at the end of this final mile of America—without
an acre of refuge remaining?

I've been moving for so long I can't remember. I've
been awake for days. From walking to car rides, to
hitchhike pick-ups, all the way back to the tour bus and
the years by motorcycle beforehand. I've crossed deserts
and mountains and valleys to bring myself here. I can't
recall precisely where I've been or what I've done.

My boots slip on the slick crag beneath me. I
anchor myself, pressing a hand against the stone, and
look over the edge of the bluff where the Atlantic Ocean
crashes onto Maine's jagged coast fifty feet below. I look
out over the water and struggle to decide what to do
next. The sirens get louder.

I know the answers must be somewhere in my
memory. I know it as well as I've ever known anything.

I remember the nightmares that tormented me every night. I remember waking each morning in panic, struggling to recognize each day's new surroundings. I wonder if my fate is to wander for all eternity.

I stare straight down at the waves crashing against the rocks below. I look toward the sky, the thumping rotors of the approaching helicopters still a few miles out of sight. The police cars are coming. I hear the television trucks behind them. I hear the groan of the angry mob as they narrow their pursuit. They want to get a piece of me. They want to exact their revenge. They want to destroy me. Others are on their way as well who are sympathetic, coming to watch in sadness. Some are just curious. They want to watch this play out, they want to see what happens next. Some are just as hopeless as I, and they come to pay their final respects. Their hearts beat on the off chance I might somehow persevere. But most of these people—the detectives in their undercover cars, the police officers in their cruisers, the newsmen in their vans, the feds in their helicopters, the vigilantes on foot—they're after my head.

They're coming. All of them. I don't have to look over my shoulder to know who they are.

I need to escape. To keep progressing forward. To move from this slick stony overhang before I'm cuffed or killed. The sirens get louder. Louder.

I look to my right, to my left. A series of ridges run along the cliff's gentler slopes. *Maybe...*

How much time do I have?

My eyes fix on the sunset, a blur of brightness where the sky appears to meet the edge of the rocky earth. The hopeless mess of my life glows red and purple and gold into the twilight. The brightness of the setting sun hits my eyes like a blow to the brain. With the overpowering light comes perfect clarity. Just the brutal truth. It all zaps bright white into my head.

That's when the sudden and loud roar of a motorcycle's engine breaks me from my trance. It roars far above the sirens, over the noise of distant helicopters, over everything. And it's getting louder.

From the recesses of my mind I see the man on the motorcycle—virile, bold, unafraid, wise, rebellious, inspirational—and for a moment I swear I see my father in his face. With the police on his tail, he races up the mountain road from around a bend, his body strong and lean, his bike shiny and chrome. Cop cars—their sirens wailing—practically nip at his rear tire as his motorcycle sputters and he shifts into third gear.

Gaining some separation, he shifts into fourth... then fifth. He speeds toward the bluff's edge. He must be going a hundred miles an hour.

Just like that, he launches off the lip of the rocky cliff, and the police cars skid to a stop. The officers leave their cars and run toward me. "Freeze! Put your hands in the air!" I make my break for it, racing along the ridge.

The man on the motorcycle soars above me. It all happens in slow motion. He's up in the sky, his chrome tailpipes glimmering like red streaks in the sunset, white lines of smoke fuming from their ends. Above them, the reflective decals on his helmet shimmer like stars in the blue sky. He's up there—bright, beautiful, everything I ever wanted to be.

I stumble and roll a few yards at a time, my pants and shirt tearing against the rocks, my arms scraping and bleeding as I continue, picking myself up each time I fall.

The man on the motorcycle plunges into the sea with a splash. I pant as I watch him hit the water.

I tumble all the way down the ridge and I'm cut. I'm bleeding, and my ragged clothes are soaked with sweat and blood.

I scramble to my feet and rush into the surf.

The sea consumes me as I approach the deeper water, and I swim further and further toward the sinking motorcycle.

Now with my arms tired and saltwater in my lungs, I take a full breath then dive down deep, looking for the bike's shiny chrome, looking for my hero's fearless face.

I surface, gasping.

Then I take another breath and submerge. Again I go under, hold my breath, search.

Nothing.

I resurface. Tears run down my cheeks, the ocean swallows me.

He must've been knocked out cold on the impact of the crash. He must've sunk to the ocean's floor with the motorcycle. He must be down there somewhere, his body falling to rest on the sandy depths where, ever so slowly, he will be stripped to his essences. In infinite molecular parts, he will rest at the ocean's floor until one day... called up by the raging waters of an epic wind, he'll rise to the surface where he'll be launched from the waves with a magnificent gust, blown once more across the

189

American continent.

I emerge from a long search below the water.

I gasp for breath and struggle to keep my lips above the surface.

From where I float in the water, I see the eastern coast of the United States. I watch as a procession of people carefully make their way down to the sands from the cliffs. They're law officers and federal agents, paramedics, reporters, cameramen. Behind them stand their elected leaders, and behind them, the masses. Some call for my head. Most just look on.

Past the beach and past the crowds, the bluffs give way to dense forest. Beyond the trees are rolling fields. Still further, occasional metropolises dot the land. More crowds stir within them. Farmhouses freckle the Great Plains, and the Rocky Mountains emerge mightily. Vast deserts spread further west, and a final set of snowcapped peaks give way to the sandy surf line that ends our country's storied frontier. Low clouds hug the snow-covered mountains. There are lakes so smooth and clear they give back the sky.

A few hundred miles down this coast, and few hundred years ago, a fleet of ships are landing on this shore. They tame its wilderness. They brutally overtake its natives. They spill blood on its soil. They found a nation on hopes and ideals. They enslave. They industrialize. They simplify. They complicate. They struggle through their own evolution.

They discover a land of opportunity, a land of sadness, a land of freedom, a land of hypocrisy, a land of hope. They discover their frontier and conquer it little by little until the silent day when every beast is slain and it suddenly seems wrong. How is this happening? I can no longer see the truth, tarnished by tall tales. *What the hell is going on?*

On the shore, the country's countless citizens stand before me. Their tragedy, their inspiration, failure, humor, anger, struggle, racism, politics, toil, education, achievement, and desire—what of it? What has it made of itself? What have I made of myself?

I look at this great stretch of land before me, at this coastline that continues for as far as I can see, and I imagine Manuel somewhere in New York City. I imagine his children who I cooked dinner for. I see this land mass and I imagine Arkansas far beyond these cliffs, and the vagrant I'd kept out of jail. I recall the thousands I entertained, the stories I created from their lives—stories to inspire, to empathize, stories about love and liberty. The random pieces of fan mail that found me all over the country, all the lives that touched me, all the souls I connected with. The lonely addicts I befriended, the homeless man to whom I loaned subway fare at the Brooklyn shelter, the smiling faces of New Orleans. The love. The heartbreak. All my failures. The seemingly endless pain. The unstoppable drive to live.

I see all the faces—the people I helped, the people who helped me. I see those faces and I smile.

I remember all those youngsters who smiled when they recognized me from the newspaper. I remember all those who helped me, all those who made my life better, all those who allowed me to do the same for them.

My eyes gush. My staggering breaths shake my frame. It's life. It seems perfect, vibrant, tragic, so hopeful. The survival of an incredible journey—I've done it! And along the way, I gained a deeper understanding of the world.

In my mind I see an aerial image of the planet, with a zoom lens gradually gaining focus on the Northern Hemisphere and getting ever closer. I see the United States of America. I see the northeast. I see Maine. I see the coast. I see myself. I see myself.

On the beach, a crowd awaits me. I have consequences to face, responsibilities I won't run from any longer. I swim to the shoreline. The water gets shallow and I can stand. Through the surf, I walk to the police, to the government, to the people. What they think of me is written on their faces and scribbled on their picket signs.

I'm not the criminal, not the hero, not any singular person they've pegged me to be. Rather I am just a man, equally capable of acting as convict or conqueror, victim or victor. That's when I realize the hidden wisdom in Sam's frustrated advice to me: "Anyone can be a hero... Just act like it."

Around me the waves pound thunderously, like a raucous ovation. I face the three hundred million people of my native soil.

As the authorities run to me, as they draw their guns and pull their handcuffs from their belts, I politely raise both my open palms above my head. I can't say that I'm giving up—not on my journey or my dreams, but I am accepting my identity and acknowledging my problems and handling them head on. I will run no more. Who I am, who I hope to become, what life will make of me—those things I'll just have to accept. I'll make the best of it.

With my palms to the sky, I feel the sea breeze catch a droplet of water from my forearm. I feel it blow from my skin. I see it sweep toward the sky, carried by the wind over the towns of the east coast, soaring over the Midwestern planes, rising above the Rocky Mountains, enduring the harsh desserts, and going on and on, up and up, higher than the peaks of Denali. I watch as it sweeps across our land, beautifully, still rising.

Acknowledgments

Thanks first to the friends I met across America from 2006 to 2011—those who were brave enough to befriend a stranger on a Greyhound bus, or a motorcyclist working odd jobs from town to town, or any of the many people I was in between. Ours became encounters often too intimate to be recorded as facts, and I know better than to leave a paper trail of names. You provided me shelter, food, often employment, and sometimes affection—but much greater still, the candid insight you lent me into your life filled me with inspiration, purpose, and courage. I hope you see yourself in this story. May it be as empowering to you as our encounters have been to me.

Thanks also to the people who unknowingly prepared me for life on the road, and for what would become an eight-year odyssey getting this book written and published. Specifically, thanks to my military friends from the University of Texas ROTC program for their friendship, wisdom, and training. Thanks to my friends from the University of Texas Athletics Department and baseball program who taught me how to turn dreams into reality. Thank you Zulfikar Ghose, my creative writing professor and a poet and author in his own right. Many an afternoon I've dreamt that I'm still eating pistachios and sipping beer by your pool.

Thanks to my attorney and old friend, without whom this book would not have been printed, distributed, or sold. Thanks to the entire team at Harbinger Book Group for seeing this through.

Finally, and most importantly, thanks to my mother, my father, and my two sisters for their faith, love, and support. May your children live adventures much greater (and much safer) than anything I could conceive.

CPSIA information can be obtained at www.ICGtesting.com
Printed in the USA
LVOW07*0719130514

385566LV00003B/7/P

9 781940 500355